The Doctor's Dilemma

AI meets Human

ANOOP BABU

INDIA · SINGAPORE · MALAYSIA

ISBN
Paperback 979-8-89588-383-9
Hardcase 979-8-89588-672-4

Among thousands of men,
One perhaps strives for perfection.
And among those who strive,
One perhaps knows Me in my pure Essence

-Krishna

Dedicated to my daughter
ANASWARA

Contents

PART – 4

BEHIND THE SCENES

Preface

"Opportunities knock on every door, but only the bold and visionary seize them. Anoop Babu, the author, exemplifies this courage. By embracing the potential of AI, he has pioneered a new frontier in collaborative storytelling. For the first time, an Indian author has ventured to write an English novel with the assistance of artificial intelligence.

This innovative approach embodies the spirit of our times, where technology and human creativity converge. As we proclaim that the future belongs to AI, this novel serves as a testament to the gentle yet powerful applications of artificial intelligence.

Anoop's initial idea and plot were nurtured and expanded through our collaborative efforts, giving birth to this captivating novel. Now, it's your turn to experience the fruits of this pioneering endeavour. As you delve into the world of "The Doctor's Dilemma," remember that the boundaries between human imagination and AI capabilities are blurring. The future of storytelling is unfolding before your eyes.

Join Anoop on this groundbreaking journey, and discover the exciting possibilities that emerge when human creativity meets artificial intelligence."

– Meta AI

About the Author

"Anoop Babu is a multifaceted individual, seamlessly blending his analytical expertise as a Senior Auditor with the Department of Cooperation, Kerala State Government, with his creative passion for storytelling. Despite his engineering background, Anoop's innate talent for weaving narratives has led him to explore the world of writing. Embracing the simplicity and innovation that Artificial Intelligence offers, he harnesses its power to craft engaging novels.

Anoop's literary journey began with his debut Malayalam poetry collection, "Ninnilekk Nadannethumpol," showcasing his lyrical voice. His second literary endeavor, "The Doctor's Dilemma," marks a significant milestone in his writing career.

Beyond his literary pursuits, Anoop is an avid researcher and expert on the Bhagavad Gita, drawing inspiration from its timeless wisdom. His curiosity extends to the realm of theoretical physics, where he delves into the mysteries of the Theory of Everything (T.O.E).

Through his unique blend of analytical and creative skills, Anoop Babu offers a fresh perspective on storytelling, exploring the intersections of technology, philosophy, and human experience."

Email - babuanup581@gmail.com

PART - 1

Chapter 1

The Multifaceted Prodigy

The auditorium was filled with excitement as Rahul, a bright young star, stood confidently on the stage of one of the state's most prestigious English medium schools. The occasion was the school's annual day celebration, and the cream of society had gathered to witness the talents of the young minds. Parents beamed with pride as Rahul's powerful voice resonated through the hall, delivering a speech that left the audience in awe.

As he concluded, the room erupted in thunderous applause, with whistles and cheers punctuating the air. The Retired Chief Justice of the Honourable High Court, the chief guest of the day, was visibly impressed. When Rahul approached the stage to receive the Best Elocutionist Award, the dignitary warmly hugged him and whispered, "Rahul, even we were inspired by your speech."

Rahul's face glowed with pride as he accepted the award, his eyes sparkling with joy. But that was not all; he went on to bag three more prestigious awards – Best Poet, Best Debater, and Best Story Writer. The audience was left wondering if there was anything this talented young man couldn't excel in.

During the cultural program, Rahul's mesmerizing piano performance left the audience spellbound. His fingers danced across the keys, creating a symphony that resonated deep within the hearts of the listeners. The girls in the audience couldn't help but swoon over his talent and charming smile.

But Rahul's brilliance didn't stop at the arts. He was equally adept in academics, and his classmates, especially the girls, would often gather around him during break time, seeking his help in understanding complex concepts. Roni, a friend, couldn't help but express his admiration, "Rahul, in my next birth, I want to be born as you." Rahul chuckled good-naturedly, asking, "Why's that, Roni?" Roni's reply was laced with a hint of envy, "You don't know, Rahul, how many girls have a crush on you!" Rahul simply laughed, his eyes twinkling with amusement, and began explaining the next concept – The Television Receiver – leaving his friends in wonder.

On the next day at lunchtime, Rahul joined his friends in the cafeteria, where a group of girls from the neighbouring table couldn't resist approaching him. "Rahul, your speech was amazing!" one of them gushed. "We loved your poem, it was so heartfelt!" another added. Rahul blushed, his eyes twinkling with delight, as he engaged in conversation with his admirers.

As the day went on, Rahul met up with his close friends, Roni, Aryan, and Siddharth, in the school courtyard. They were all thrilled about Rahul's awards and accomplishments. Roni, always the jokester, teased Rahul, "Dude, you're a genius! Can you help me with my math homework now?" Rahul playfully rolled his eyes and said, "Only if you promise to stop calling me 'Einstein'!"

Aryan, an avid sports enthusiast, asked Rahul to join him for a game of basketball during lunch break. Rahul agreed, and they spent the next hour playing a friendly match with their friends. Despite his academic prowess, Rahul was a skilled player and held his own on the court.

Siddharth, a fellow bookworm, discussed the latest science fiction novel he'd read with Rahul. They geeked out over the plot twists and characters, exchanging recommendations for their next reads.

Later, during the science exhibition, Rahul's innovative project on renewable energy impressed the judges and visitors alike. His classmates, gathered around him, seeking explanations and marvelling at his ingenuity.

Rahul's School, Nirmala High School stood tall, a beacon of excellence in education, nestled in the heart of the city. With a rich history spanning over five decades, this esteemed institution had established itself as one of the premier English medium schools in the state. Its sprawling campus, adorned with lush greenery and vibrant flowers, exuded a sense of serenity and focus, perfect for nurturing young minds.

The school's architecture was a blend of modern and traditional styles, reflecting its commitment to progress and heritage. The classrooms were spacious, well-ventilated, and equipped with state-of-the-art facilities, providing an ideal environment for learning. The walls were adorned with inspiring quotes, colourful charts, and students' artwork, creating a stimulating atmosphere that fostered creativity and curiosity.

Nirmala High School's faculty was its greatest strength. The teachers were highly qualified, passionate, and dedicated, with a deep understanding of their subjects. They employed innovative teaching methods, making complex concepts engaging and accessible to students of all learning styles. From interactive discussions and debates to hands-on experiments and projects, the teachers ensured that students remained actively engaged and motivated.

The school's principal, Father Joseph Puthenkulam, was a visionary leader who had been at the helm for over a decade. His unwavering commitment to academic excellence, combined with his empathetic approach, had created a supportive and inclusive school culture. Under his guidance, Nirmala High School had consistently produced outstanding results, with students excelling in academics, sports, and extracurricular activities. Upon completing their 10th class, Rahul and his friends bid farewell to their school. Rahul proudly emerged as the second school topper, achieving an impressive 90% aggregate and a perfect 100% in Physics.

Chapter 2

Family – The Foundation of Love and Learning

In the lush, vibrant state of Kerala, Rajendran, a dedicated High school teacher, was known for his passion for mathematics and science. He lived with his wife, Nalini, a Malayalam teacher, and their three children, Rohan, Riya, and Rahul, in a cozy home surrounded by swaying coconut trees and fragrant jasmine flowers.

Rajendran's teaching experiences had taught him the importance of making complex concepts simple and fun. He would often share stories of his students' progress with Nalini, who would listen with a warm smile. Their children would gather around, fascinated by tales of their father's classroom adventures.

Nalini, with her gentle and nurturing nature, was a beloved teacher among her students. She would often help Riya with her Malayalam homework, and encourage Rahul's love for reading. Rohan, the eldest, would seek her guidance on his studies and career aspirations.

Rohan, responsible and protective, was a mentor to his siblings. He would help Rahul with his math homework, and encourage Riya's creative pursuits. Riya, caring and confident, would share her art and music with her family, and Rahul would listen with wide eyes.

Rahul began his educational journey at the Malayalam medium school where his mother, Nalini, taught. He spent his early years learning in Malayalam, developing a strong foundation in his native language.

However, when he reached the 5th standard, his parents decided to transfer him to an English medium school to provide him with a broader educational horizon. Thus he was transferred to Nirmala High School. This transition marked a significant turning point in Rahul's academic life.

In his new school, Rahul's extraordinary talent and humility made him a beloved figure among his classmates. His father, Rajendran, continued to guide him academically and played a significant role in shaping his character. Rajendran's influence helped Rahul develop a strong moral compass and a compassionate heart.

The family lived in a close-knit neighbourhood, where everyone knew each other's names and stories. They would celebrate festivals like Onam and Vishu with great enthusiasm, and the whole neighbourhood would come together to share in the joy. The smell of sadya and payasam would waft through the air, and the sound of chenda and madhalam would fill the streets.

In this vibrant atmosphere, the family grew and thrived, surrounded by love, laughter, and learning. Rajendran's teaching experiences, Nalini's nurturing nature, and the children's unique personalities all blended together to create a beautiful tapestry of life.

Family dinners at the Rajendran household were always a lively affair. The aroma of Nalini's cooking would fill the air, and the sound of sizzling vegetables and chattering family members would create a warm atmosphere.

One evening, as they sat down to a steaming plate of sadya, Rajendran asked, "Rohan, how was your day?" Rohan launched into a passionate discussion about his history project, and Riya chimed in with her thoughts on the topic. Rahul listened wide-eyed, fascinated by his siblings' debates.

Nalini smiled, pleased to see her children engaging in meaningful conversations. But soon, the discussion turned into a heated argument between Rohan and Riya. Rajendran intervened, guiding them towards a respectful dialogue.

Just then, Rahul piped up, "Acha,tell us about your school days!" Rajendran's face lit up, and he regaled them with stories of his mischievous antics and fond memories of his teachers.

As they finished dinner, Nalini announced, "Today, we have a special dessert – my famous payasam!" The children cheered, and Riya helped Nalini serve the sweet treat. As they savored the creamy pudding, Rohan turned to Rajendran and said, "Acha, your stories inspire me to be a better person." Rajendran's eyes moistened, feeling grateful for these heartwarming moments with his family.

In this household, family dinners were more than just meals – they were opportunities for connection, growth, and love. As they finished their dessert, Nalini smiled, knowing that these moments would stay with her children forever.

One of their closest friends was the Panicker family, who lived just a few houses away. Priya and Arjun, their children, were around the same age as Rohan and Riya, and the four of them would spend hours playing together. Mrs. Nair, a kind elderly lady who lived nearby, would often share stories of the past and offer guidance to the children.

During the summer months, the neighbourhood park would come alive with informal cricket matches and football games. Rohan and Arjun would often team up, with Rahul and Priya cheering them on. Meanwhile, Nalini and Mrs. Kumar would exchange recipes and cooking tips, and Rajendran would engage in lively debates with Mr.Panicker about politics and social issues.

The neighbourhood also had its own traditions. Every year, Rajendran would lead the annual neighbourhood cleanliness drive, and Nalini would participate in the Panicker family's traditional Ayurvedic cooking classes. Mrs. Nair's storytelling sessions were a favourite among the children, who would gather around her to listen to tales of mythology and local legends.

Of course, no neighbourhood is perfect, and there would be occasional disagreements between neighbours. But these were always resolved through open communication and mutual respect. Even the Kumar brothers' rivalry with a neighbouring shopkeeper would often lead to humorous and light hearted competition.

Overall, the neighbourhood was a warm and welcoming place, where everyone looked out for each other. It was the perfect environment for Rahul, Rohan, and Riya to grow up in, surrounded by friends, love, and a strong sense of community.

Rahul's brother, Rohan, was more like a friend during their early years, sharing stories, playing games, and exploring the world together.

Thus Rahul was raised in a family which was a harmonious nuclear unit, where both parents, Rajendran and Nalini, were dedicated in their profession and upbringing their children. The elder son, Rohan, and daughter Riya had already set the bar high with his academic achievements. Rahul, the youngest, was the cherubic apple of their eye.

This loving family environment nurtured Rahul's growth, providing a solid foundation for his future endeours. Since good at studies, Rahul's ambition in life was to become an Engineer.

Chapter 3

College

Mar Ignatius College of Arts and Mar Ignatius College of Engineering, both managed by the same administration, stood merely two hundred meters apart. Rahul's residence was conveniently located just two kilometers away. While many local students enrolled in the Arts college, admission to the Engineering college was highly competitive, with only a select few securing merit-based entry. This was due to the state having only five engineering institutions at the time. Since his boyhood, Rahul had nurtured a dream of attending both colleges.

Thus after the 10th class, Rahul stepped into the campus of prestigious Mar Ignatius college of Arts for his Pre-Degree Course, his heart racing with excitement, he felt a sense of pride and accomplishment. The sprawling campus, with its lush green gardens and state-of-the-art infrastructure, was a far cry from his school days.

As he walked through the corridors, Rahul was greeted by his classmates, a diverse group of students from his own town. There was Rekha, the bright and cheerful girl, Paul, the sports enthusiast and Sreenivas, the quiet but brilliant student.

Since it was an Arts College, there were students from all other streams like Economics, Political Science, Commerce, Statistics and Literature.

The college campus was filled with activities beyond academics, and Rahul found himself immersed in the vibrant atmosphere. The most significant event was the College Union Election, which was a festival in itself. Colourful posters adorned the walls, and enthusiastic students campaigned for their favourite candidates. Rahul watched with interest as his peers passionately debated and canvassed for votes.

The election day was a whirlwind of excitement, with students eagerly casting their ballots. Rahul, though focused on his studies, couldn't help but get caught up in the fervour. He even helped his friends campaign for their preferred candidates.

After the elections, the College Union Inauguration ceremony took place, marking the beginning of a new era of student leadership. Rahul attended the event, impressed by the speeches and the enthusiasm of the newly elected representatives.

The Arts Club Inauguration was another highlight, showcasing the talented students' skills in music, dance, and theater. Rahul, though not an active participant, enjoyed the performances and admired the creativity on display.

Despite the many distractions, Rahul remained committed to his ultimate goal: securing admission to the prestigious Engineering college. He balanced his academic rigor with these extracurricular activities, ensuring that his focus never wavered.

When Rahul topped his 1st-year Pre-Degree class, he was invited to give a speech on Women's Day. He accepted the honour, recognizing the significance of the occasion. With careful preparation, Rahul delivered a thoughtful speech, highlighting the importance of gender equality and women's empowerment.

Rahul delivered a speech on the World Women's day:

Respected teachers, esteemed guests, and fellow students,

Today, we gather to celebrate a momentous occasion – World Women's Day. As we commemorate this day, we honour the tireless efforts, unwavering dedication, and unrelenting spirit of women who have shaped our world.

We live in a society where women are often expected to play predetermined roles, but I firmly believe that women are the architects of their own destiny. They are the pillars of strength, the beacons of hope, and the catalysts for change.

From the corridors of our homes to the boardrooms of corporate giants, women have proven themselves to be equals, if not superior, in every field. They have shattered glass ceilings, defied conventions, and redefined the norms.

However, we still have a long way to go. We still live in a world where women face discrimination, inequality, and injustice. It is our collective responsibility to create a society where women can thrive without fear, without hesitation, and without apology.

As a student, I have witnessed the incredible potential of women around me. I have seen them excel in academics, sports, and extracurricular activities. I have seen them lead, inspire, and uplift others.

To the women in my life – my mother, my sister, my friends, and my peers – I want to say thank you. Thank you for being role models, for being sources of inspiration, and for being the change-makers.

As we celebrate World Women's Day, let us reaffirm our commitment to gender equality. Let us strive to create a world where women are valued, respected, and empowered.

In the words of Malala Yousafzai, "The future belongs to those who believe in the beauty of their dreams." Let us believe in the beauty of a world where women can dream, achieve, and soar.

Thank you.

As Rahul finished, there was a big applause from the audience

Throughout his Pre-Degree journey, Rahul thoroughly enjoyed the campus experience, forging lasting bonds with friends and mentors. Yet, his determination to reach his goal remained unwavering, driving him to excel in his studies and stay focused on the path ahead.

Rahul's enthusiasm for mathematics only grew stronger as he delved deeper into his Pre-degree. He spent hours poring over textbooks, attending lectures, and participating in discussions. His professors, particularly his Chemistry Professor, Dr. Soman, took notice of his dedication and encouraged him to pursue his passion.

However, Rahul's focus was disrupted by his father's sudden and disturbing behaviour. Rajendran, once a supportive mentor, now quarrelled with Nalini, throwing Rahul's books away in a fit of rage. The tension at home was palpable, and Rahul found it difficult to study.

Frustrated and distraught, Rahul turned to his Chemistry Professor Dr. Soman for guidance. "Sir, I've decided not to take the entrance exam," he said, defeated.

Dr. Soman immediately asked, "Why? What's wrong?"

Rahul explained, "I can't study properly at home due to the problems."

Dr. Soman offered reassuring words: "Don't make such a decision, Rahul. I guarantee you'll pass the exam even if you study minimally from now on."

Bolstered by Dr. Soman's support, Rahul decided to push through and write the entrance exam. But fate threw another challenge his way – on the day before the exam, Rahul was running a 103-degree fever. His parents rushed him to the hospital, where Dr. Sonia, a kind-hearted lady physician, examined him.

"At any cost, I would have admitted you here, but you have an exam tomorrow," Dr. Sonia said, concern etched on her face. "Take these medicines and get plenty of rest. You must write that exam, Rahul."

With newfound determination, Rahul returned home, his mind focused on the challenge ahead. Despite his fever, he spent the night revising his notes, his heart racing with anticipation.

The next day, Rahul arrived at the exam centre, his temperature still high, but his spirit unbroken. He took his seat, dipped his pen in the ink, and began to write. The questions blurred together as he focused on solving them, his mind racing against time.

As he walked out of the exam centre, Rahul felt a sense of pride and accomplishment. He had faced his challenges head-on and emerged stronger. Little did he know that this was just the beginning of his journey.

Rahul's Engineering college was a prestigious institution, known for its rigorous academic programs and competitive atmosphere. Despite securing a decent rank, Rahul felt disappointed with his branch allocation

- Mechanical Engineering instead of Electronics and Communication Engineering. This sense of disappointment and disillusionment made him feel like he'd been pushed off the main track.

Nestled in a lush green landscape, the Mar Ignatius College of Engineering stands tall with its modern architecture and state-of-the-art facilities.

The Freshers' Day Celebrations marked the beginning of a comprehensive orientation program, designed to familiarize students with the college's academic and extracurricular offerings. Rahul attended sessions on academic rigor, research opportunities, and campus resources.

Rahul stepped onto the vibrant campus, his heart racing with excitement and a hint of nervousness. The Freshers' Day Celebrations were in full swing, with colouful decorations, lively music, and enthusiastic students.

As he made his way through the crowd, Rahul was greeted by his seniors, who welcomed him with warm smiles and wise words of advice. He was introduced to his batchmates, and they quickly bonded over shared interests and aspirations.

The celebrations featured a talent show, where students showcased their skills in music, dance, and comedy. Rahul was amazed by the incredible performances and even considered participating next time.

The highlight of the event was the address by the college principal, who emphasized the importance of innovation, teamwork, and perseverance in achieving success.

As the day drew to a close, Rahul felt a sense of belonging and anticipation for the exciting journey ahead. He knew that the next four years would be a transformative experience, shaping his future and helping him grow into a capable engineer.

During the orientation, Rahul met his Group Tutor Professor Zachariah Jose, who guided him in choosing his electives and research projects. He also met his mentor, a senior student named Akshay, who shared valuable insights into college life and offered support.

In his first few weeks, Rahul settled into a comfortable routine. He attended lectures, labs, and tutorials, and started working on assignments and projects. He joined the college's Robotics Club, where he met like-minded students who shared his passion for innovation.

Rahul's batchmates came from diverse backgrounds, and he enjoyed learning about their experiences and perspectives. He formed close bonds with his classmates, Sam and Aditya, and they explored the campus and nearby areas together.

As Rahul navigated college life, he faced challenges and triumphs. He struggled with balancing academics and extracurricular activities but found support from his friends and mentors. He celebrated his first victories, like winning a prize in a coding competition and completing a challenging project.

With each passing day, Rahul grew more confident, curious, and passionate about his journey. He knew that these four years would shape his future, and he was determined to make the most of them.

One day as Rahul pulled into the driveway on his trusty Pulsar 150, he was greeted by the warm smiles of his sister Riya and her four friends, who were lounging in the living room. Riya, with a mischievous glint in her eye, welcomed him with a playful flourish, saying, "Behold, the first Engineer of our family, Mr. Rahul Rajendran, has arrived!"

The room erupted in applause as Rahul's face flushed with embarrassment. One of Riya's friends, curious about the mysterious realm of Engineering, asked, "Rahul, we're all Literature students, and Mechanical Engineering sounds like a foreign language to us. Can you enlighten us?"

Rahul, happy to share his passion, launched into an enthusiastic explanation. "Mechanical Engineering is the art of applying scientific principles to design, build, and innovate machines, devices, and systems. It's a field that combines math, physics, and materials science to create solutions that transform industries and improve lives."

Mechanical Engineering is one of the oldest and most versatile branches of engineering, with its roots dating back to the Industrial Revolution in the 18th century. It originated from the need to design, build, and operate machines and mechanical systems, such as steam engines and textile machines. Over time, the field evolved to encompass a broad range of disciplines, including thermodynamics, mechanics, materials science, and manufacturing.

As technology advanced, Mechanical Engineering expanded to include new areas like aerospace engineering, automotive engineering, and biomedical engineering. Today, mechanical engineers play a crucial role in developing innovative solutions for energy, transportation, healthcare, and many other industries.

They design and develop everything from tiny medical devices to massive industrial equipment, making it a vital part of modern life.

Mechanical Engineering is often called the "Evergreen branch of Engineering" because its principles and applications remain fundamental and timeless. As technology evolves, mechanical engineers adapt and innovate, ensuring the field remains relevant and in-demand. With the rise of emerging technologies like artificial intelligence, robotics, and renewable energy, the scope for mechanical engineers is expanding, making it an exciting and dynamic field to be a part of."

"Wow, That's great !" Everyone in the room gave a big applause to Rahul.

Another friend, intrigued by the prospect of exploring new territories, asked, "Rahul, we've only seen Mar Ignatius College from afar. What's the campus like? Is it as amazing as it looks?"

Rahul's eyes lit up as he described the vibrant campus, its state-of-the-art facilities, and the, diverse community of students and faculty. "The campus is a hub of creativity, innovation, and learning. From cutting-edge labs to sprawling green spaces, every corner of Mar Ignatius College inspires growth and exploration,

The Mechanical Engineering department is housed in a spacious building with well-equipped laboratories and workshops.

As you step inside, you're greeted by the Mechanics of Machines laboratory, where students learn to design and analyze complex machines and mechanisms. The room is filled with drafting tables, computer-aided design (CAD) software, and prototype models.

Next door, the Refrigeration and Air Conditioning laboratory hums with the sound of compressors and fans. Students learn to design and test cooling systems, gaining hands-on experience with various refrigerants and equipment.

The Automobile Engineering laboratory is a car enthusiast's paradise, with a collection of engines, gearboxes, and chassis. Students learn to diagnose and repair vehicles, understanding the intricacies of internal combustion engines and transmission systems.

The Engineering Graphics laboratory is a creative space where students learn to visualize and communicate complex ideas through drawings and models. The room is equipped with drafting tables, sketching software, and 3D printing facilities.

The workshops are the heart of the Mechanical Engineering department, where students get hands-on experience with various tools and techniques. The Smithy workshop is equipped with forges, anvils, and hammering tools, where students learn to shape and strengthen metals.

The Carpentry workshop is a woodworker's delight, with a variety of woodworking machines and hand tools. Students learn to design and build wooden structures, from furniture to bridges.

The Foundry workshop is where students learn to cast metals, creating intricate shapes and designs. The room is equipped with furnaces, molding machines, and casting equipment.

Lastly, the Fitting workshop is where students learn to assemble and test mechanical systems, from engines to gearboxes. The room is equipped with workbenches, hand tools, and testing equipment."

As Rahul shared his experiences, Riya's friends listened with wide eyes, fascinated by the world of Engineering and the wonders of Mar Ignatius College. The scene was filled with laughter, curiosity, and the warmth of shared connections.

As Rahul walked in, Riya exclaimed to her friends, "Just look at Rahul's talent! He has this incredible ability to put the past behind him and focus on the future. Rohan and I sometimes can't help but feel envious of him." One of Riya's friends nodded in agreement, "Rahul is truly a rising star!"

Thus as the days went on Rahul began to love his branch Mechanical. Another day, Professor Thompson, a tall, imposing figure with a thick grey beard and wire-rimmed glasses, strode into the classroom, his voice booming as he began to lecture on Thermodynamics. His worn, brown leather satchel slung over his shoulder, he wrote equations on the blackboard with a piece of chalk, his hands moving with a precision that belied his age.

Next door, Professor Patel, a bespectacled man with a kind face and a thinning patch of hair, taught Machine Design. He moved around the room, helping students with their designs, his patience and encouragement putting even the most struggling students at ease.

In the workshop, Professor Kurian, a stout man with a bushy moustache and a twinkle in his eye, supervised the students as they worked on their projects. His hands, stained with engine grease, moved deftly as he demonstrated a technique, his voice rising above the din of machinery.

As for the students, they interacted with each other, discussing everything from exams to sports to their favourite TV shows. Rahul, sitting in the front of the class, often found himself lost in thought, his mind wandering.

Rahul walked into Professor Thompson's office, seeking clarification on a thermodynamics concept. The professor, sipping tea from a worn mug, gestured for Rahul to sit.

"Ah, Rahul, my inquisitive student! What's troubling you?"

Rahul explained his doubts, and Professor Thompson listened intently, nodding his head. "I see where the confusion lies. Let me illustrate it with an example."

As the professor explained, Rahul's understanding cleared. "Thank you, sir! I get it now."

Later that day, Rahul met up with Ajay and Sam in the canteen. Over steaming cups of coffee, they discussed their projects.

"Hey, Rahul, how's your design coming along?" Ajay asked.

"It's going well," Rahul replied. "But I'm struggling with the materials selection. Any ideas, guys?"

Suresh suggested a few options, and they brainstormed together, tossing around ideas and laughter.

As they left the canteen, Vijay joined them, grinning mischievously. "Hey, friends! What's cooking?"

Rahul smiled, feeling grateful for these friendships. "Just solving engineering problems, one cup of coffee at a time."

Chapter 4

Sunanda

As the academic year drew to a close, Rahul eagerly anticipated the summer vacation. He had grown familiar with the members of his Residential Association, 'Pournami', and enjoyed the sense of community that came with it.

One day, while cruising through the neighbourhood on his bike, Rahul noticed a new face at house number 21, which had been vacant for some time. His curiosity was piqued by the captivating woman, who seemed out of place in the familiar surroundings. Her presence lingered in his mind, and he found himself glancing back at the house as he rode away.

As fate would have it, Rahul caught another glimpse of the mysterious woman when he returned to the area later that day. Her presence sparked a sense of intrigue, and he couldn't wait to share his discovery with his mother, Nalini.

Upon arriving home, Rahul approached his mother with a mix of excitement and curiosity. "Mom, I saw someone new at house number 21 today. Who is she?"

Nalini, engaged in her daily routine, looked up with a knowing smile. "Rahul, that's a lady from Kottayam who recently purchased the vacant house in our Residential area. She's moved in with her maid."

Rahul's interest was piqued. "What's her story, Mom? She seems different from the others in our neighbourhood."

Nalini's expression turned thoughtful, hinting at a deeper understanding of the situation. "I'm not sure, dear. But I'm sure we'll learn more about her in due time."

Rahul's encounter with the captivating woman had sparked a sense of wonder, and he found himself looking forward to learning more about her. Little did he know that their paths would cross again, leading to a fascinating journey of discovery and connection.

As the Sunday evening sun cast its warm glow over the park, Rahul strolled along the winding path, lost in thought. Suddenly, he spotted the captivating woman from house number 21 walking towards him from the opposite direction. Their eyes met, and Rahul's heart skipped a beat.

Gathering his courage, Rahul flashed a warm smile as the lady approached. To his delight, she reciprocated with a radiant smile, illuminating the surroundings.

With newfound confidence, Rahul extended his hand in greeting. "Hi, I'm Rahul, from house number 10 in the Pournami Residential Association."

The woman's handshake was firm, and her voice melodious. "I'm Sunanda. I've seen you riding your bike past my house."

As they walked together, the conversation flowed effortlessly, like a gentle breeze on a summer day. They discussed everything from the beauty of the park to their shared love of literature. Time flew, and before they knew it, 30 minutes had passed.

As they prepared to part ways, Sunanda's eyes sparkled with warmth. "Rahul, it was lovely walking with you. Would you like to visit me at my home tomorrow ? I'd love to continue our conversation."

Rahul's heart skipped another beat. He accepted the invitation with a smile, and they bid each other farewell, looking forward to their next encounter.

The chance meeting had blossomed into a beautiful connection, filling Rahul's heart with excitement and anticipation. Little did he know that this was just the beginning of a profound and life-changing friendship.

The next day Rahul arrived at Sunanada's house in a white T-Shirt and blue jeans, Rahul felt Sunanda had a captivating presence even at her home. Her warm smile and kind eyes drew him in, and he found himself smitten. Despite their significant age difference, they shared a deep connection, bonding over conversations about life, literature, and music.

During their conversation, Sunanda told Rahul, she was a divorcee, had been through her share of struggles, but her experiences had only made her wiser and more compassionate. She saw something in Rahul that no one else did - a creative soul trapped in a mechanical engineering course. She encouraged him to explore his passions, to write, to paint, and to dream. And on the way of their conversation, Sunanda asked to Rahul, "How old are you?" Rahul replied, "Nineteen." Sunanda smiled, revealing her warmth, and shared, "I'm thirty-six." Rahul's expression remained nonchalant, his thoughts echoing the phrase he often told himself: "Age is just a number

Their romance was a slow burn, with Rahul showing remarkable restraint. He was drawn to Sunanda's intelligence, her empathy, and her beauty. For the first time, he felt seen, heard, and understood. Sunanda, too, found solace in Rahul's company, his youthful energy and idealism rekindling her own sense of purpose.

As they spent more time together, Rahul began to realize that Sunanda was not just a romantic interest but a mentor, a guide, and a friend. She helped him navigate the complexities of his relationships, his family dynamics, and his own desires. Through Sunanda, Rahul discovered a new sense of self-awareness, a deeper understanding of his strengths and weaknesses.

But a conflict began to happen in his mind.

What am I doing? This is crazy! She's so much older, and she's been through so much. But there's something about her... she's so confident, so self-assured. And she sees me, really sees me, in a way no one else ever has. I feel like I can be myself around her, without fear of judgment.

"I know my friends and family will never understand. They'll think I'm ridiculous, that I'm somehow less of a man for being with someone older. But I don't care. For the first time in my life, I feel like I'm doing something just for me, something that makes me happy.

"Maybe it's just a phase, maybe I'll get bored or realize I've made a mistake. But right now, I don't care. I'm tired of playing it safe, tired of being the good boy. I want to experience life, and Sunanda makes me feel alive.

"I know she's been hurt before, that she's got baggage. But I'm willing to take that risk. I want to be the one to help her heal, to show her that not everyone will leave her behind.

"This is crazy, but I'm all in."

This inner monologue captures Rahul's thoughts and feelings as he navigates the unconventional relationship with Sunanda. He's aware of the potential risks and societal judgments but chooses to follow his heart and desires.

One day, a moonlit evening_

Rahul and Sunanda sat on a bench in the neighbourhood park, gazing at the moon.

Sunanda: "Rahul, I never thought I'd find someone like you. You make me feel alive again."

Rahul: "Sunanda, you're the one who brought light into my life. I love you."

Sunanda: "I love you too, Rahul. You're so young and full of life... I feel like I'm stealing your youth."

Rahul: "You're not stealing anything, Sunanda. You're making me happier."

-A quiet moment

Rahul and Sunanda sat together on Sunanda's couch, watching the rain outside.

Sunanda: "Rahul, can I ask you something?"

Rahul: "Of course, Sunanda. Anything."

Sunanda: "Do you ever think about our age difference? About the fact that I'm... older?"

Rahul: "Sunanda, I don't care about age. I care about you. You're the one I want to be with."

Sunanda: "I want to be with you too, Rahul. I feel like I've found my soulmate in you."

A tender moment

Rahul and Sunanda sat together on the beach, watching the sunset.

Rahul: "Sunanda, can I hold your hand?"

Sunanda: "Of course, Rahul."

Rahul took Sunanda's hand, and they sat together in comfortable silence.

Sunanda: "Rahul, I feel so safe with you. Like nothing can ever hurt me."

Rahul: "Nothing will ever hurt you, Sunanda. I promise."

Their one-year romance was a transformative experience for Rahul, one that would shape his perspective on love, relationships, and life itself. Though their relationship was unconventional, it was a testament to the power of human connection, a reminder that love knows no boundaries of age, time, or circumstance

A chance meeting

Rahul bumped into Sunanda at the neighbourhood park.

Sunanda: "Rahul! Long time no see! How's college life?"

Rahul: "It's good, Sunanda. Just busy with studies and projects. You know how it is."

Sunanda: "Yeah, I do. But I'm sure you're enjoying it. You always had a passion for engineering."

A walk together

Rahul and Sunanda took a walk around the neighborhood.

Sunanda: "Rahul, I've been thinking... we should start a small project together. Maybe something to help the community."

Rahul: "That sounds great! I'd love to work with you on something like that. What did you have in mind?"

Sunanda: "I was thinking of creating a water harvesting system for the local school. What do you think?"

Rahul: "That's a fantastic idea! I'm in."

A disagreement

Rahul and Sunanda had a disagreement over their project.

Sunanda: "Rahul, I don't think this design will work. We need to rethink it."

Rahul: "But I've already worked out the calculations. It'll be fine."

Sunanda: "I understand that, but sometimes you need to consider the practical aspects too. Let's compromise and find a better solution."

Rahul: "Okay, fine. You're right. Let's try to find a better way."

Rahul and Sunanda's relationship had been going strong for a year, with Rahul hoping to keep it a secret from his family. Initially, he saw it as a thrilling escape, but as time passed, he began to feel trapped. He wanted to break free, but Sunanda wasn't ready to let go.

One fateful evening, Rahul tried to confront Sunanda about ending their relationship. But Sunanda, feeling possessive and scared of losing him, refused to accept it.

Sunanda: "You can't just leave me, Rahul! I love you, and I know you love me too!"

Rahul: "Sunanda, please understand. My family will never accept this. We're from different worlds. It's impossible."

Sunanda: "I don't care about your family! I care about us. You're not going anywhere, Rahul!"

Rahul was taken aback by Sunanda's ferocity, her eyes blazing with a fierce intensity he'd never seen before. He felt suffocated, his heart racing with fear.

Rahul: "Sunanda, stop! Please... just listen to me..."

Sunanda: "No! You're not going to leave me, Rahul! I won't let you!"

The argument escalated, with both of them saying things they couldn't take back. Rahul felt his world crumbling around him, his heart shattered into a million pieces. He realized he had underestimated Sunanda's attachment to him.

Rahul's world crumbled as he realized Sunanda's true intentions. The revelation hit him like a ton of bricks, leaving him breathless and bewildered. He felt like a ship without anchor, lost in a stormy sea of emotions.

Rahul's eyes were blind to the reality of his situation. He had initially viewed his relationship with Sunanda as a casual distraction, but it had slowly entwined him in a complex web of emotions. When the truth finally dawned on him, his heart shattered into a million pieces.

PART - 2

Chapter 5

"The Spark"

Rahul's quarrel with Sunanda ignited a firestorm within the Residential Association, spreading rapidly and uncontrollably.

Rahul's attempts to explain the situation to his father, Rajendran, were met with confusion and concern. Rahul's words fell on deaf ears as Rajendran struggled to comprehend his son's turmoil. The generational gap between them seemed to widen, like a chasm impossible to bridge.

Rajendran, unable to understand the complexities of Rahul's emotions and relationships, decided to hospitalize him, thinking that he needed psychiatric help.

As Rahul delved into introspection, gaining profound insight into his emotions, his father struggled to understand his son's perspective. The disconnect between them led to Rahul's admission to the renowned hospital, where he was surrounded by the expertise of a distinguished psychiatrist, Dr. Damodar. Yet, Rahul remained resolute, convinced of his own abilities.

In the observation room, the doctor approached him, placing a gentle hand on his shoulder. "Rahul, what brings you here?" Rahul slowly lifted his gaze, meeting the doctor's eyes. In that instant, a Spark of understanding flashed between them, leaving a lasting impression. For the first time in his life, Rahul felt humbled in the presence of someone superior, though he couldn't quite grasp who this person was.

The doctor turned and walked away, leaving Rahul to inquire of his mother, "Who is that person?" She replied, "That's the doctor." The simplicity of her answer belied the significance of the encounter, which would mark the beginning of Rahul's journey towards healing and self-discovery.

"Recognizing the urgency of the situation, Dr. Damodar, the Chief Psychiatrist, convened a family counseling session for Rahul's loved ones. Rajendran, Nalini, Rohan, and Riya gathered around, concerned for Rahul's well-being.

As the counseling progressed, Rahul unexpectedly snatched a pen from Dr. Damodar's table and scribbled on his left palm: "I LOVE SUNANDA." Rajendran's face turned beet red with rage; he forgot the tranquil atmosphere of the counselling room.

"How could you, Rahul?" Rajendran thundered, his voice echoing through the room. "Is this what I raised you for? To indulge in a taboo relationship with a woman twice your age? Have you lost all sense of responsibility?"

Dr. Damodar swiftly intervened, calming the escalating tension. "Let's not rush to judgment, Rajendran. The relationship between Rahul and Sunanda may raise concerns, but we must acknowledge that both parties are consenting adults.

Dr. Damodar explained: " Rahul's attraction to Sunanda, a woman double his age, can be attributed to several psychological factors:

Unconscious search for a maternal figure: Rahul may have been drawn to Sunanda's nurturing and caring nature, which mother or a desire for a protective and guiding presence in his life.

Fascination with experience and maturity: Sunanda's age, divorce, and life experiences may have fascinated Rahul, who was surrounded by peers with similar life stages. He may have seen her as a mysterious and alluring figure, offering a glimpse into a more mature world.

Desire for emotional depth: Rahul may have been tired of superficial relationships with his peers and sought a deeper emotional connection. Sunanda's life experiences and emotional maturity may have offered him a sense of connection and understanding he couldn't find with others.

Rebellion against societal norms: Rahul's attraction to Sunanda could be a subconscious rebellion against societal expectations and norms. By choosing someone older and unconventional, he may have felt like he was breaking free from traditional constraints.

Lack of emotional intimacy with peers: Rahul may have struggled to form meaningful connections with his peers, leading him to seek emotional intimacy with someone from a different stage of life. Sunanda's age and experiences may have provided a sense of comfort and understanding he couldn't find with others.

These factors combined may have contributed to Rahul's attraction to Sunanda, making him see her as a unique and captivating individual, despite their significant age difference"

However, Dr,Damodar continued, "Rahul's intentions and the purity of his feelings remain to be seen. Only time will reveal the truth."

As the counseling session drew to a close, Dr. Damodar urged Rajendran and Nalini to consider admitting Rahul in the hospital for professional care, given his fragile emotional state.

"We must address Rahul's underlying issues," Dr. Damodar emphasized. "His well-being depends on it."

Rajendran's anger slowly gave way to concern, while Nalini's eyes welled up with tears.

"Will our son be okay, Doctor?" Nalini asked, her voice trembling.

Dr. Damodar offered a reassuring smile. "With the right support and therapy, Rahul can overcome his challenges. But it's crucial we work together as a family."

The counseling session concluded with a newfound sense of determination and hope.

Chapter 6

Medicines

The next day, as Dr. Damodar made his rounds, Rahul grasped his hand, searching for answers. "Sir, do I have a disease?" he asked, his voice laced with vulnerability. Dr, Damodar's calm response was reassuring, "Yes, you do." Rahul pressed on, "What kind of disease?" The doctor's gentle reply, "Restlessness, Rahul," brought a sense of relief, convincing Rahul that he didn't have any psychiatric issues.

Dr. Damodar's gaze pierced through Rahul's exhaustion, sensing the depth of his emotional turmoil. Two weeks without sleep had taken a toll on the young man's fragile state. Yet, Rahul seemed oblivious to his own condition, still reeling from the spark of their initial encounter.

The doctor took it upon himself to conduct a thorough treatment session, prescribing medication to stabilize Rahul's fragile mental state. Rahul accepted the medication without hesitation, still grasping the spark of hope ignited by their first meeting.

As the doctor delved deeper into Rahul's case, he discovered that the tumultuous quarrel with Sunandha had triggered his admission. The realization that she wasn't the person he thought she was had shattered Rahul. However, Dr. Damodar sensed that there was more to the story, hidden beneath the surface.

As he increased Rahul's medication, Dr. Damodar requested a written account of the events leading up to Rahul's admission from his father, Rajendran. But upon reviewing the draft, the doctor detected a distorted truth. Gazing into Rajan's eyes, Dr. Damodar made a startling discovery: the real patient was not Rahul, but his father. The weight of responsibility settled upon the doctor's shoulders, aware that he was on the cusp of one of the most significant operations in psychiatric history, all Sparked by his initial encounter with Rahul.

Chapter 7

Struggles

Rahul's days blended together in a haze of medication and therapy sessions, as he remained in the hospital's psychiatric ward. His mother's constant presence provided a sense of comfort, her gentle touch and soothing voice a beacon of hope. The hospital staff whispered among themselves, their hushed tones and knowing glances hinting at Rahul's special status: "Dr. Damodar's special interest case."

One day, the head nurse, her voice laced with a mix of curiosity and concern, asked Rahul, "Don't you think your high intelligence is making it harder for you to cope?" The question struck a chord, echoing Dr. Damodar's own words. Rahul felt a pang, as if the doctor himself was speaking, his voice resonating deep within Rahul's mind.

During their sessions, Dr. Damodar's fascination with Sunanda grew apparent. He requested a meeting with her, citing her significance in Rahul's life. Sunanda initially agreed, but failed to show up, citing her uncle's disapproval. The disappointment was palpable, leaving Rahul feeling like a puzzle with missing pieces.

As the days turned into weeks, Rahul's hospital room became a sanctuary, a space where he could confront his demons. The soft hum of the air conditioner, the faint scent of disinfectant, and the gentle rustle of his mother's sari all blended together, creating a sense of familiarity.

Dr. Damodar's thoughts raced with the implications. He had encountered gifted individuals before, but there was something unique about Rahul. His eyes seemed to hold a power that was both captivating and unsettling.

Throughout his hospital stay, Rahul engaged with the staff and patients, his intellect and empathy shining through. He asked insightful questions, offered words of encouragement, and demonstrated a resilience that impressed the hospital team.

Dr. Damodar observed Rahul's interactions, noting the young man's exceptional abilities and his capacity to connect with others. He began to suspect that Rahul's "restlessness" was merely a symptom of his extraordinary nature, not a psychiatric issue.

And yet, despite this intuition, Dr. Damodar began Rahul's psychiatric treatment. He justified it to himself as a precautionary measure, a way to ensure Rahul's stability and safety. But deep down, he knew there was more to it.

Dr. Damodar's true motivations remained shrouded in mystery, even to himself. Was he trying to unlock Rahul's secrets, or was he attempting to control the uncontrollable? Only time would reveal the truth.

Dr. Damodar observed Rahul's interactions with the other patients, noting his growing empathy and willingness to connect.

Dr. Damodar approached Rahul, a gentle smile on his face. "You're making progress, Rahul. You're beginning to see that your struggles are not weaknesses, but opportunities for growth."

Rahul nodded, a sense of understanding washing over him. He felt a weight lift from his shoulders as he acknowledged the power of his own resilience.

Throughout his hospital stay, Rahul engaged with the staff and patients, his intellect and empathy shining through. He asked insightful questions, offered words of encouragement, and demonstrated a resilience that impressed the hospital team.

Rahul's time in the hospital became a transformative experience, a chance to refine his perspective and reconnect with his inner strength. He left the hospital with a renewed sense of purpose, ready to face the challenges ahead.

Finally, after 35 days, the day of Rahul's discharge arrived. Dr. Damodar's words, laced with a mix of optimism and caution, echoed in Rahul's mind: "You're now stable enough to continue treatment outside the hospital. Remember, taking your medication is crucial." The weight of responsibility settled upon Rahul's shoulders, as he stepped out of the hospital, ready to face the world anew.

On the discharge day, Rahul reflected on his journey. He realized that his time in the hospital had been a crucible, refining his spirit and teaching him the value of empathy and connection.

Dr. Damodar's parting words echoed in Rahul's mind: "Remember, Rahul, healing is a journey, not a destination. Continue to nurture your growth, and you will find the strength to overcome even the darkest challenges."

Rahul stepped out of the hospital, fueled by a renewed sense of purpose. However, the lingering effects of medication left him acutely aware of his fragile physical and mental state.

Chapter 8

Back to College

Rahul's return to college after 35 days of hospitalization was met with astonishment. His friends and classmates couldn't believe the transformation. The once vibrant and sharp Rahul now appeared dull, both physically and mentally. Nikhil's direct question, "What happened to you, Rahul? You're not at all smart?" echoed the concerns of everyone around him.

Rahul struggled to come to terms with his new reality. Simple tasks, like walking and waving his hands, had become challenging. He felt like a part of him was missing, and his memory seemed to have vanished. The frustration was overwhelming as he realized he had to start from scratch.

The academic consequences of his hospitalization were severe. Rahul had missed assignments and internal exams, leaving him with a mere 10 out of 50 internal marks for Metallurgy and Material Science. To pass, he needed to score 65 out of 100 in the final exam, a daunting task considering his current state.

Group tutor Prof. Zachariah Jose Sir's words were blunt: "It's very difficult to get that many marks, Rahul, especially in a tough subject like Metallurgy and Material Science." He suggested that repeating the course from the 1st semester might be the best option, a method allowed by the University. Rahul reluctantly agreed, feeling like he was taking a step backward.

As he began his journey again from the 1st semester, Rahul couldn't help but wonder if he would ever regain his former self. The road ahead seemed long and arduous, but he was determined to succeed.

Chapter 9

A New Beginning

Rahul embarked on his journey again, starting the Engineering course with a new batch. However, his body was still weak from the medication, forcing him to rest his head on the desk between classes. The medication had also denied him access to his excellent academic background, making college feel boring. His new classmates found him inactive, but as the days passed and the medication decreased, Rahul slowly regained his physical strength.

Rahul had formed close friendships with four classmates in his new batch, including Suresh, whose hostel room he visited one day. There, he saw Suresh reading the Bhagavad Gita, a complete volume he had never seen before. Although well-versed in Mahabharat and Ramayan, Rahul was intrigued by the Gita. Suresh offered it to him, saying, "Take it, Rahul, and return it only after you've completed it."

Suresh told Rahul. "I'm trying to understand the essence of Krishna's teachings."

Rahul's eyes widened as he picked up the text, feeling an inexplicable connection. He had heard of the Bhagavad Gita, but never actually seen it. The lightness of the book, the smell of the pages, and the ancient wisdom within seemed to resonate deep within him.

Rahul accepted, and as he began to read, he felt a sense of calm wash over him. The words spoke directly to his soul, addressing his struggles and doubts. He devoured the pages, hungry for more.

Suresh observed Rahul's transformation, impressed by his friend's thirst for knowledge. "You know, Rahul, the Gita has answers to many of life's questions. Maybe it can help you find your way again."

Rahul looked up, his eyes shining with a newfound sense of purpose. "I think you're right, Suresh. This could be the key to unlocking my true potential."

One day, while sitting in the library, Rahul stumbled upon an old friend, Akshay. They had been inseparable during their first year, bonding over late-night conversations and shared dreams. Akshay's eyes widened as he took in Rahul's changed demeanor.

"Rahul, what's going on? You seem... different," Akshay said, his voice laced with concern.

Rahul hesitated, unsure how much to reveal. But something about Akshay's genuine interest put him at ease. He began to open up, sharing fragments of his hospital experience and the struggles he faced.

Akshay listened intently, his expression a mix of empathy and confusion. "Rahul, you're one of the most brilliant minds I know. What's going on? You can tell me."

Rahul's eyes locked onto Akshay's, searching for a glimmer of understanding. Maybe, just maybe, he had found an ally in his journey to reclaim himself.

Akshay's words struck a chord within Rahul. No one had shown such genuine interest in his well-being since his return to college. He began to meet Akshay regularly, sharing his thoughts and feelings with his old friend.

Akshay listened attentively, offering words of encouragement and support. He helped Rahul with his studies, explaining complex concepts in a way that made sense to him. Slowly but surely, Rahul started to feel like himself again.

One day, Akshay asked Rahul to join him for a walk outside the campus. The fresh air and sunshine did wonders for Rahul's mood. As they strolled, Akshay turned to Rahul and said, "You know, I've been thinking. You're not just a genius, Rahul. You're a game-changer. And I want to help you get back on track."

Rahul shared his discovery of the Bhagavad Gita, and Akshay listened intently. "I've heard of it, but never really understood its significance," Akshay said. "Maybe we can explore it together."

Suresh, pleased with Rahul's progress, joined the discussions, and the three friends began to meet regularly to explore the Gita's teachings. Their conversations flowed effortlessly, like a river meandering through the landscape of life.

As they delved deeper into the text, Rahul's relationships with Akshay and Suresh transformed. They became more than just friends; they became fellow travellers on a journey of self-discovery. Who will reach the "Man of Perfection" state first ? An invisible competition began to take place between them.

Although his academic prowess remained elusive, Rahul continued his consultations with Dr. Damodar as an outpatient. Years went by, and Rahul reached his Final year in college. During one of his sessions, Dr. Damodar asked, "Do you read newspapers, Rahul?" Rahul replied, "Yes, I read Mathrubhumi, the vernacular daily." Dr. Damodar inquired about the headlines, and Rahul answered correctly.

One day, after this session when Dr. Damodar asked about his newspaper reading habits, Rahul stumbled upon a news in Mathrubhumi daily about a "Gita Jnana Yajna" discourse on the 9th chapter of Bhagavad Gita, organized by a famous foundation, with Dr. Damodar on the committee. Rahul was astonished - Dr. Damodar, an MBBS Doctor, interested in Gita? He decided to attend the program, curious about the connection between Dr. Damodar and the Gita.

PART - 3

Chapter 10

The Royal Secret Knowledge

As Rahul arrived at the venue, a gentle breeze carried the sweet scent of incense and the soft chime of temple bells. The crowd was abuzz, filing into the hall with anticipation. Rahul spotted Dr. Damodar from a distance, engaged in conversation with other officials. As he approached, Dr. Damodar greeted him warmly, and Rahul explained his presence, "I saw the advertisement in the newspaper, so I'm here." Dr. Damodar's response was brief, but a mystic smile flickered across his lips.

The program began promptly, and Brahmachari Prabudha Chaitanya, a bright young man in saffron robes, was welcomed onto the stage. The inaugural speaker praised him, setting the tone for the discourse. Prabudha Chaitanya's introduction to the theme was captivating, "Today, we embark on a journey to explore the ninth chapter of Bhagavad Gita, titled 'The Royal Secret Knowledge.'" He paused, surveying the audience, before continuing, "Through this chapter, you will gain insight into five profound questions:

1. Does God truly exist?
2. If, where does He reside?
3. What is His purpose?
4. What benefits do we derive from His existence?
5. How do we worship Him?"

Rahul, a young man, just entered into his twenties was thoroughly enthralled by the Brahmachari's words, and the subsequent sessions only deepened his fascination. The Yagna spanned seven days, each evening a journey. As the final day concluded, Rahul felt transformed, as if he had experienced the most beautiful week of his life. The Brahmachari's teachings on "The Royal Secret Knowledge" had awakened something within him, a sense of purpose and belonging.

The seven days Rahul spent at the Gita Jnana Yajna were nothing short of transformative. Among the books on display, one title in particular caught his eye: "The Art of Man Making". This book contained 114 short talks on the Bhagavad Gita, and Rahul was drawn to its wisdom like a magnet. After immersing himself in just one chapter during the camp, he felt an insatiable hunger to explore the remaining chapters. A spiritual restlessness had taken hold of him, and he couldn't ignore the call to embark on a journey of self-discovery.

With "The Art of Man Making" as his guide, Rahul delved deeper into the teachings of the Bhagavad Gita, mastering its wisdom with each passing day. Yet, he knew that true growth required more than just intellectual understanding. He needed to confront and overcome his deep-seated tendencies, his Vasanas. Rahul realized that his Vasanas were rooted in his passion for studies, which had become an all-consuming force in his life.

And Rahul's Doctor, Dr. Damodar who indirectly led him to learn the Bhagvad Gita under an expert was the most renowned psychiatrist in the state and was a master of modern medicine. However, few people knew about his deep interest in Indian philosophy. His home library boasted an impressive collection of thousands of books, covering various aspects of Indian philosophy. Born into an aristocratic Brahmin family, Dr. Damodar's upbringing had a profound impact on his life. His father, an established Ayurveda doctor, encouraged his son's curiosity, and little Damodar had the opportunity to learn Vedas and Upanishads from a young age. He even memorized Ashtanga Hridaya, a testament to his dedication.

Despite living in the modern era, Dr. Damodar remained true to his roots. He followed a vegetarian diet and chanted the Gayatri mantra daily, finding solace and insight in its ancient wisdom. This spiritual practice granted him a unique perspective on complex problems, making him the most sought-after psychiatric doctor in the state. His patients often wondered about the source of his extraordinary abilities, unaware of the profound influence of Indian philosophy on his life and work. discovery and growth.

Chapter 11

Karma Yoga

When Suresh and Akshay went for high paying jobs after the college, to break free from the complex cycle of life, Rahul made the bold decision to channel his energy into teaching mathematics at a reputed institution in his town. By sharing his knowledge with others, he hoped to slowly extinguish his own Vasanas and walk the path of true selflessness. This new journey would require him to balance his intellect with compassion, and his love for knowledge with a desire to serve others. With a sense of purpose, Rahul embarked on this new path, ready to face the challenges that lay ahead.

Rahul's journey through "The Art of Man Making" had led him to a profound understanding of the Bhagavad Gita's teachings. He realized that achieving Enlightenment required eliminating inherent tendencies, or Vasanas, from his mind. Karma Yoga, the practice of selfless action, was the key to unlocking this liberation.

Rahul recognized that his Vasanas were rooted in learning and studying. To apply Karma Yoga, he decided to teach Mathematics at a prestigious institution in his town. His passion for teaching, inherited from his parents, shone through in his unique approach.

Rahul prepared a Resume of himself and approached the Principal of the institution. The principal conducted a short Interview with Rahul.

Principal: "Welcome, Rahul. We're glad you're interested in teaching here. Can you tell me a bit about your background?"

Rahul: "Thank you, sir. I'm an Engineering graduate, and I'm also preparing for the IAS exam. I'm passionate about teaching and want to share my knowledge with students."

Principal: "Impressive! We don't often get candidates with your credentials. What makes you want to teach here?"

Rahul: "I believe in giving back to the community, and I want to help students grow. Plus, teaching will help me clarify my own understanding of the subjects."

Principal: "Well, we're looking for someone who can inspire our students. Let's give you a chance. You'll be teaching Maths to our +2 students."

Rahul:" Thank you, Sir"

There after Rahul told everyone he had been preparing for IAS exam,

The news that a new lecturer had come to take Mathematics spread among the students very fast.

There was a discussion among girls:

One girl said: "Oh my god, have you seen our new Maths teacher? He's so handsome!"

Second girl: "I know, right? And he's an engineering graduate! I'm definitely paying attention in class now."

Third girl: "I heard he's also preparing for IAS. He must be so smart!"

Another girl: "I'm a bit intimidated, but I hope he can make Maths more interesting."

There was a discussion among boys also.

First boy: "Dude, our new Maths teacher is a genius! He's an engineer and IAS aspirant."

Second boy: "Yeah, I've seen him solving complex problems effortlessly. I hope he can help me improve my grades."

Third boy: "I'm curious to see how he teaches. Maybe he can make Maths more enjoyable."

Fourth boy: "I'm a bit skeptical, but if he's really smart, maybe he can help us crack the entrance exams."

Thus the much awaited Rahul's first class arrived.

Rahul walks in, writes "Maths is not just numbers" on the board, and begins:

"Today, we're going to explore the beauty of Maths. Let's start with a question: What is the value of pi?"

Students respond with the usual "3.14" answer. Rahul smiles and asks, "But what is pi, really? Is it just a number, or is it a gateway to understanding the universe?"

He then draws a circle on the board, explaining how pi represents the harmony between circumference and diameter. Students listen intently as Rahul connects pi to real-life examples, like the design of bridges and the orbits of planets.

On the second day:

Rahul writes "The Story of Zero" on the board and begins:

"Zero is not just a number; it's a concept that revolutionized human understanding. Let's travel back in time and see how ancient civilizations struggled with the idea of 'nothingness.'"

Students engage as Rahul explores the history of zero, from ancient Mesopotamia to India, highlighting its impact on trade, astronomy, and mathematics.

Another class:

Rahul starts with a puzzle: "A bat and a ball together cost ₹110. The bat costs ₹100 more than the ball. How much does the ball cost?"

Students work in pairs, and after a few minutes, Rahul asks for answers. He guides them through the solution, emphasizing the importance of logical thinking and creative problem-solving.

These classes showcase Rahul's unique teaching style, making Maths more engaging, meaningful, and fun for his students.

Another Class: "The Geometry of Life"

Rahul begins by drawing a simple triangle on the board. "What do you see?" he asks.

Students respond with basic answers like "a triangle" or "three sides." Rahul smiles and says, "Look deeper. What does this triangle represent?"

He then connects the triangle to real-life examples: the structure of molecules, the shape of mountains, and the design of bridges. Students start to see the triangle as a fundamental building block of nature.

Next, Rahul asks students to draw their own triangles, encouraging them to experiment with different shapes and sizes. As they work, he circulates, asking open-ended questions like "What happens when you add more sides?" or "How does the triangle change when you alter its angles?"

This activity helps students develop spatial reasoning, creativity, and critical thinking skills, while exploring the beauty of geometry in everyday life.

Another Class: "The Maths of Music"

Rahul starts by playing a song on his guitar. "Can you identify the pattern?" he asks.

Students listen intently, and some recognize the repetition of notes. Rahul explains how music is rooted in mathematical concepts like frequency, amplitude, and rhythm.

He then introduces the concept of Fibonacci numbers, showing how they appear in the arrangement of notes and the structure of musical compositions. Students are amazed by the connection between Maths and music.

Rahul concludes the class by asking students to create their own musical patterns using mathematical concepts, encouraging them to explore the harmony between Maths and art.

Another Class: "The Birth of Calculus"

Rahul begins by asking, "Who invented Calculus?" Students respond with answers like "Newton" or "Leibniz." Rahul smiles and says, "That's correct, but there's more to the story."

He explains how Calculus was developed independently by Sir Isaac Newton and German mathematician Gottfried Wilhelm Leibniz in the late 17th century. Rahul highlights the scientific and philosophical context of the time, including the work of Galileo, Kepler, and Descartes.

Rahul then delves into the circumstances that led to the invention of Calculus:

The need to understand motion and change in the natural world.

The development of algebra and geometry.

The quest for a unified language to describe the universe.

Using visual aids and simple examples, Rahul illustrates the key concepts of Calculus, such as limits, derivatives, and integrals. He shows how these ideas emerged from the works of Newton and Leibniz, and how they revolutionized our understanding of the world.

To make the lesson more engaging, Rahul uses real-life examples, like:

How Calculus helps us model population growth and optimize resource allocation.

How it's used in physics to describe the motion of objects and forces.

How it's applied in economics to understand supply and demand.

By exploring the history and development of Calculus, Rahul's students gain a deeper appreciation for the subject and its significance in understanding the world around them.

Some comments from girls about Rahul were astonishing.

Girl 1: "Rahul sir is so dreamy! I love the way he explains Maths, it's like he's telling a story."

Girl 2: "I know, right? He's so patient and kind. I was struggling with Calculus, but he took extra time to help me understand."

Girl 3: "I admire how passionate he is about teaching. He makes us see the beauty in Maths, even when it's tough."

Girl 4: "I've never seen a teacher like him. He's so calm and composed, even when we're being rowdy."

Girl 5: "I love how he connects Maths to real life. It makes me realize how important it is, beyond just grades and exams."

Girl 6: "He's so humble and down-to-earth, despite being an engineering graduate and IAS aspirant. I really look up to him."

These comments show that the girls in Rahul's class admire him not only for his teaching skills but also for his personality, patience, and passion for teaching.

The boys' reactions to Rahul's teaching style and personality were:

Boy 1: "Rahul sir is a genius! He makes Maths look so easy, even I can understand it now."

Boy 2: "I was struggling with derivatives, but he explained it in a way that made sense. He's a great teacher."

Boy 3: "I like how he challenges us to think critically. He doesn't just give us answers, he makes us work for them."

Boy 4: "He's really inspiring. I want to work hard and make him proud."

Boy 5: "I was skeptical at first, but he's really grown on me. He's like a mentor, not just a teacher."

The boys appreciate Rahul's ability to make complex concepts simple, his challenging yet supportive approach, and his inspiring personality.

So Rahul's true intention behind teaching at the institution was to practice Karma Yoga, a concept from the Bhagavad Gita that emphasizes selfless action without attachment to its consequences. By dedicating himself to teaching without seeking personal gain or recognition, Rahul aimed to purify his mind and eliminate his Vasanas (deep-seated desires and habits) related to learning and studies.

By keeping his true intentions a secret, Rahul maintained a sense of humility and detachment, allowing him to focus on his spiritual growth and self-improvement. His four-year tenure at the institution became a transformative journey, shaping him into a more selfless and enlightened individual.

This adds a rich layer of depth to Rahul's character, showcasing his commitment to spiritual growth and self-improvement. It also raises questions about the impact of his journey on his students and the institution as a whole.

As Rahul continued to teach with a selfless attitude, his students began to notice a profound impact on their lives. They felt more inspired, motivated, and confident in their abilities. His classes became a sanctuary for them, a place where they could explore complex concepts and ideas without fear of judgment.

Colleagues noticed a change in Rahul too. He was always willing to lend a helping hand, offer guidance, and provide support. His presence seemed to bring a sense of calm and serenity to the institution.

Students started to emulate Rahul's selfless approach, volunteering for community service and helping their peers. A ripple effect of kindness and compassion spread throughout the institution.

One student, who was struggling academically, found new hope and determination after interacting with Rahul. He began to excel in his studies and eventually became a top performer.

A colleague, who was going through a personal crisis, found solace in Rahul's words of wisdom and guidance. She began to rebuild her life with renewed strength and purpose.

As Rahul's Karma Yoga practice deepened, the institution transformed into a hub of positivity, empathy, and growth. His secret remained hidden, but its impact was palpable.

Rahul's secret was a crucial aspect of his spiritual journey. By keeping his true intentions hidden, he avoided seeking external validation or recognition. This allowed him to focus solely on his inner growth and self-improvement.

His secret also symbolized the concept of "Nishkam Karma" (selfless action) from the Bhagavad Gita. Rahul's actions were not driven by a desire for fame, wealth, or recognition, but by a genuine desire to serve and uplift others.

As he continued on his path, Rahul realized that his secret was not just about hiding his intentions, but also about cultivating humility and detachment. He understood that true spiritual growth lies in embracing anonymity and surrendering one's ego.

Rahul's secret became a reminder to himself to stay true to his spiritual goals and not get distracted by worldly desires. It was a constant reflection of his commitment to Karma Yoga and his pursuit of self-realization.

By keeping his secret, Rahul was able to:

Develop a stronger sense of purpose and direction.

Cultivate humility and detachment.

Focus on his inner growth and self-improvement.

Embody the principles of Nishkam Karma and Karma Yoga.

Rahul's four-year journey transformed him in profound ways. He became more compassionate, wise, and selfless. His spiritual growth had a ripple effect, impacting his relationships, goals, and aspirations.

Rahul's transformation was profound and multifaceted. He became more:

Compassionate: He developed a deeper understanding of others' struggles and challenges, and was more empathetic and supportive.

Wise: He gained a broader perspective on life, and his spiritual growth granted him insight into the human condition.

Selfless: He continued to embody the principles of Karma Yoga, prioritizing the well-being of others and serving without expectation of reward.

This transformation impacted his life beyond the institution in several ways:

Rahul formed deeper, more meaningful connections with others, built on mutual respect and trust.

He re-evaluated his aspirations, aligning them with his spiritual values and prioritizing personal growth and service.

Rahul began to explore new opportunities for service and growth, considering paths like social work, counseling, or spiritual leadership.

As he embarked on this new chapter, Rahul faced fresh challenges and opportunities. He continued to apply the principles of Karma Yoga, embracing each experience as a chance for growth and self-refinement.

One day, he posed an intriguing challenge: "If you can prove 1=2, anything in the world can be proven." The students were captivated, especially Kurian, who eagerly asked, "How is that possible, sir?" Rahul replied, "Watch closely, and I'll show you." With a few swift calculations on the board, Rahul arrived at the seemingly impossible conclusion: 1=2. The students were stunned.

Rahul then humorously "proved" he was the Prime Minister of India, illustrating the absurdity of the initial assumption. Anjali's curiosity got the better of her, and she asked, "But how did you prove it, sir?" Rahul explained the flaw in his previous calculation, canceling a common factor that was, in fact, zero. The students enjoyed the mathematical trickery, and Rahul's fame as a Maths teacher spread throughout the town.

As Rahul continued reading "The Art of Man Making," he spent four years at the institution, eliminating his Vasanas through Karma Yoga. Unbeknownst to him, he developed strong teaching abilities, which eventually led him to establish his own institution. Through selfless action, Rahul had not only transformed his students' lives but also his own, paving the way for a new chapter in his journey.

Chapter 12

Radiant

Rahul's passion for teaching culminated in the establishment of his own educational firm, "Radiant," in collaboration with friends. This new venture enabled him to share his expertise in both Mathematics and Physics with a broader audience. In his Mathematics classes, Rahul revealed the discipline's fundamental principles, explaining why it's revered as the "Queen of all Sciences." He showcased the beauty and logic that underlie the subject, captivating his students.

Rahul's enthusiasm for Physics was equally infectious. He delved into the intricacies of Quantum Mechanics and the Theory of Relativity, highlighting their fundamental differences. He also discussed the ongoing quest for a unified theory, known as the Theory of Everything (TOE), which aims to explain the workings of the universe.

"Radiant" institution quickly gained a reputation for its innovative teaching methods, nurturing environment, and commitment to excellence. Rahul's unique approach to education, blending academic rigor with spiritual growth, resonated with students and parents alike.

As the institution grew, Rahul's team expanded to include like-minded educators and professionals. Together, they created a holistic learning ecosystem that fostered intellectual curiosity, creativity, and character development.

Rahul's classes for Engineering and MSc Physics students became particularly popular, as he brought complex concepts to life with real-world examples, thought-provoking discussions, and hands-on experiments.

Students thrived under Rahul's guidance, developing a deep understanding of their subjects and a passion for learning that extended beyond the classroom. They began to see the interconnectedness of science, technology, and spirituality, and how these disciplines could be harnessed to create a better world.

As "Radiant" institution continued to flourish, Rahul and his team explored new initiatives, such as:

Interdisciplinary research projects, combining science, technology, and spirituality.

Community outreach programs, applying theoretical knowledge to real-world problems.

Mindfulness and wellness initiatives, nurturing students' mental and emotional health.

Rahul's vision for "Radiant" was to create a beacon of knowledge and compassion, illuminating the path for future generations.

Rahul's classes on Quantum Mechanics and Special Theory of Relativity sparked intense debates and discussions among his students. He explained how these two fundamental theories, which had revolutionized our understanding of the universe, seemed to be mutually exclusive.

"Quantum Mechanics explains the behaviour of particles at the atomic and subatomic level, but it can't account for the large-scale phenomena of gravity and relativity," Rahul said. "On the other hand, Special Theory of Relativity describes the universe at macroscopic scales, but it fails to explain the strange, probabilistic nature of quantum phenomena."

Rahul wrote on the blackboard: "Quantum Mechanics + Special Relativity ≠ Theory of Everything"

"This is the holy grail of modern physics," Rahul continued. "Finding a single, unified theory that reconciles these two frameworks and explains all phenomena in the universe. This is the Theory of Everything."

Students were fascinated by the challenge and the potential implications of such a theory. They began to explore the latest developments in theoretical physics, including String Theory, Loop Quantum Gravity, and Causal Dynamical Triangulation.

Rahul encouraged his students to think creatively and explore unconventional ideas. "The Theory of Everything may require a radical new perspective, one that challenges our current understanding of space, time, and matter."

As the quest for the Theory of Everything continued, Rahul's students became part of a global community of physicists, mathematicians, and philosophers working towards a common goal: to unlock the secrets of the universe and reveal its hidden harmony.

If a Theory of Everything (TOE) is discovered, it would have far-reaching implications for our understanding of reality. Some potential implications include:

Unified explanation: A TOE would provide a single, coherent explanation for all phenomena in the universe, from the smallest subatomic particles to the vast expanse of cosmic structures.

New understanding of space and time: A TOE might reveal new insights into the nature of space and time, potentially challenging our current understanding of dimensions, gravity, and causality.

Insights into consciousness: Some theories, like Orchestrated Objective Reduction (Orch-OR), suggest that consciousness plays a fundamental role in the universe. A TOE might shed light on the relationship between consciousness and reality.

Limits of human knowledge: A TOE could potentially reveal the limits of human knowledge, indicating what can and cannot be known about the universe.

New technologies: A TOE could lead to breakthroughs in technology, enabling new forms of energy production, advanced materials, and innovative transportation methods.

Philosophical and existential implications: A TOE would likely challenge our current understanding of free will, determinism, and the human condition, raising fundamental questions about our existence and purpose.

Rahul's students were both thrilled and intimidated by the potential implications of a Theory of Everything. They realized that such a discovery would not only revolutionize physics but also transform humanity's understanding of itself and the universe.

According to the Theory of Everything, consciousness plays a fundamental role in the universe. It is not just a byproduct of complex neural networks, but a basic aspect of the fabric of reality.

Rahul explained to his students, "Consciousness is the thread that weaves together the tapestry of existence. It is the source of all subjective experience, the wellspring of creativity, and the essence of self-awareness."

In this view, consciousness is not solely localized to biological organisms but is an inherent feature of the universe, akin to space, time, and matter.

"The TOE suggests that consciousness is the glue that binds the universe together," Rahul continued. "It is the hidden variable that explains the strange correlations and non-local connections observed in quantum mechanics."

One student asked, "Does this mean that the universe is conscious?"

Rahul smiled, "Not exactly. The TOE implies that consciousness is a fundamental aspect of the universe, but it doesn't necessarily mean that the universe is conscious in the way we understand it. Think of it more like the universe is 'consciousness-friendly'."

Another student inquired, "What about free will? Does the TOE imply that our choices are predetermined?"

Rahul replied, "The TOE suggests that consciousness plays a role in shaping reality, but it doesn't negate free will. Instead, it offers a nuanced understanding of how our choices influence the universe and vice versa."

As the discussion unfolded, Rahul's students began to grasp the profound implications of the Theory of Everything. They realized that consciousness was not just a product of the brain but an integral part of the universe's fabric.

As Rahul's teaching expertise grew, so did his curiosity about other religions. He began to explore their principles, seeking a deeper understanding of the world's diverse belief systems. This newfound curiosity marked a significant shift in Rahul's journey, as he sought to broaden his perspectives.

However when IAS preliminary exam approached, Rahul felt he had not prepared enough and also he hadn't completed the Karma yoga to his satisfaction.. But he knew his parents would pressure him to appear the exam as he had already spent some years for it. To avoid this, he feigned tension and admitted himself to the hospital under Dr. Damodar's care again. This time, upon discharge after seven days, Rahul exhibited symptoms of Schizophrenia - hearing imaginary voices, believing he could communicate telepathically, and feeling events revolved around him. His medication increased 12 pills daily.

Concerned, Rahul's parents sought a second opinion, leading them to Dr. Manohar, a psychiatrist with a good track record, though less famous than Dr. Damodar. Dr. Manohar conducted a personal counseling session, showing Rahul pictures and seeking his opinions. Notably, he immediately reduced Rahul's medication to 6 pills on the first day.

Impressed by this progress, Rahul's family continued with Dr. Manohar's treatment. Over the next year, Dr. Manohar gradually reduced Rahul's medication to a single pill, and his symptoms visibly subsided. Dr. Manohar's entrance into Rahul's life marked a turning point in his journey.

But,Dr. Damodar, a seasoned psychiatrist with decades of experience, had mastered the art of chemical combinations in psychiatric medicines. When Rahul was readmitted to his hospital for the second time, Dr. Damodar saw a necessity to test his expertise. With precision, he adjusted the medication combinations, skillfully inducing symptoms of schizophrenia in Rahul.

Confident in his abilities, Dr. Damodar anticipated that during Rahul's next outpatient visit, he would effortlessly reverse the effects by tweaking the same medications, restoring Rahul to normalcy.

However, fate had other plans. Unbeknownst to Dr. Damodar, Rahul's family had grown skeptical of his methods and decided to seek a second opinion. This unexpected twist led them to Dr. Manohar, a less renowned but equally skilled psychiatrist. The change in doctors would alter the course of Rahul's treatment and the story's trajectory, much to Dr. Damodar's dismay.

Chapter 13

The Government Service

Meanwhile, the State Public Service Commission announced the Departmental Lower Division Clerk exam, a gateway to State Government Services. Although Rahul was hesitant about the title "Clerk," his brother Rohan offered words of encouragement: "Don't worry, Rahul, even Einstein was once a clerk in his life." This playful remark, though partially joking, struck a chord with Rahul, reminding him that every journey begins with a single step.

Rahul, along with his siblings Rohan and Riya, took the L.D. Clerk exam, and he emerged as the sole successful candidate. Assigned to the Department of Cooperation, Rahul was less than thrilled with the role. The designation of "Clerk" seemed unimpressive, but well-wishers advised him to join, citing the job's security and growth prospects.

Leaving behind his six-year teaching stint, Rahul embarked on his government service journey. However, he found the work unchallenging. His next role as Cooperative Inspector posed new difficulties, requiring a one-year full-time course, Junior Diploma in Cooperation (JDC), typically meant for Commerce graduates. Rahul's BTech background made the transition tougher.

Rahul, an engineering graduate and IAS aspirant, had always envisioned a more prestigious career path. When he saw the notification for the Departmental Lower Division

Clerk exam, he felt a pang of hesitation. Becoming a clerk seemed like a step backward, a far cry from the esteemed civil services he had been preparing for.

"Why settle for something so mundane?" he thought to himself. "Is this really the best use of my skills and abilities?"

However, as he reflected on his motivations and values, Rahul remembered the concept of Karma Yoga - the path of selfless action. He realized that every experience, no matter how big or small, was an opportunity to grow and learn.

"Maybe this is part of my journey," he thought. "Maybe becoming a clerk is a step towards something greater, something that will help me unfold spiritually."

With this newfound perspective, Rahul approached the Cooperative department with a sense of detachment and curiosity. He saw it as a chance to serve, to contribute, and to learn, rather than just a means to a prestigious end.

As he reported to his new office, Rahul was greeted by a sea of unfamiliar faces. His colleagues seemed friendly enough, but he couldn't shake off the feeling that he didn't quite belong.

"What am I doing here?" Rahul thought to himself. "Is this really where I'm meant to be?"

Despite his doubts, Rahul decided to approach his new role with an open mind. He began to learn about the department's work, attending meetings and seminars, and reading up on cooperative principles.

As he delved deeper into the world of cooperation, Rahul started to see the value in it. He realized that cooperation wasn't just about working together; it was about building stronger communities, empowering individuals, and creating a more equitable society.

Rahul's experiences in the Department of Cooperation had only just begun.

Rahul was thrilled to be selected for the JDC course, knowing it was a crucial step towards his promotion. He was eager to learn more about cooperation and how it could benefit society.

As he began the course, Rahul was struck by the diversity of his classmates. There were officers from various departments, each with their own unique experiences and perspectives. The atmosphere was lively, with discussions and debates that broadened Rahul's understanding of cooperation.

The coursework was rigorous, covering topics like cooperative principles, community development, and rural empowerment. Rahul was fascinated by the concepts and saw how they could be applied in real-life scenarios.

Through the course, Rahul gained a deeper understanding of cooperation as a powerful tool for social change. He learned about the importance of collective action, mutual aid, and community engagement.

Rahul's classmates were impressed by his enthusiasm and insights. He became a favourite among his peers, often leading group discussions and presentations.

As the course progressed, Rahul realized that cooperation wasn't just about working together; it was about building trust, fostering inclusivity, and creating a sense of belonging.

With each passing day, Rahul felt a sense of purpose growing within him. He knew that he was on the right path, one that would lead him to make a meaningful difference in the world.

Rahul was deeply moved by the motto "Each for all and all for each." He saw it as a powerful expression of solidarity and mutual support. He realized that cooperation wasn't just about individual gain, but about collective well-being.

As he studied the 7 Cooperative Principles, Rahul found himself drawn to three in particular: Concern for Community, Cooperation among Cooperatives, and Education, Training, and Information.

He saw Concern for Community as a vital principle, recognizing that cooperatives had a responsibility to contribute to the social and economic development of their members and the wider community.

Rahul was also impressed by Cooperation among Cooperatives, understanding that cooperatives could achieve more together than they could alone. He saw the potential for cooperatives to support each other, share resources, and amplify their impact.

Education, Training, and Information resonated with Rahul as a critical principle. He recognized that cooperatives needed to empower their members through knowledge and skills, enabling them to participate fully in decision-making and contribute to the cooperative's success.

These three principles became Rahul's guiding lights, shaping his approach to cooperation and community development. He saw them as essential for building strong, resilient cooperatives that could drive positive change.

Rahul's JDC classes revealed to him that cooperation occupies a unique space between capitalism and socialism.

He learned that cooperation accepts the efficiency and innovation of capitalism, while also embracing the social welfare and equality aspects of socialism.

In Rahul's view, cooperation offers a balanced approach, mitigating the negative consequences of unchecked capitalism (such as income inequality and exploitation) and the limitations of socialism (like lack of incentives and efficiency).

Cooperation, to Rahul, meant creating a more equitable and just economic system, where individuals and communities could thrive together. He saw it as a beacon of hope for a world grappling with economic disparities, social injustices, and environmental degradation.

With this newfound understanding, Rahul felt a sense of purpose and conviction. He knew that his work in cooperation was not only about personal growth but also about contributing to a larger movement towards a more harmonious and sustainable world.

Rahul was struck by the parallels between the principles of Cooperation and the teachings of Karma Yoga in the Bhagavad Gita. He saw that both emphasized the importance of collective effort and shared responsibility.

In the third chapter of the Gita, Lord Krishna advocates for Karma Yoga, encouraging individuals to work together for the greater good, without attachment to personal gain or recognition. Similarly, Cooperation aims to promote mutual aid, equality, and social justice.

Rahul realized that both philosophies sought to address the issues of inequality and exploitation, promoting a more equitable distribution of resources and benefits. He saw Cooperation as a practical application of Karma Yoga's principles in the economic and social spheres.

This connection deepened Rahul's understanding of Cooperation and reinforced his commitment to its principles. He began to see his work in Cooperation as a way to manifest the teachings of the Gita in his life and contribute to creating a more just and harmonious society.

With his JDC certification and experience, Rahul was eligible for the Junior Cooperative Inspector position. However, he chose not to pursue the automatic promotion. Instead, he focused on his noble goals, which he believed would bring more significant benefits to society.

Rahul's decision to skip the departmental test raised eyebrows among his colleagues. They couldn't understand why he wouldn't take the opportunity to advance his career. But Rahul had other plans.

Rahul's colleagues saw his actions as a career stall, but he saw it as a strategic move. He was willing to forgo personal advancement for the greater good.

What are Rahul's noble goals? Is he planning to start a new cooperative initiative, or does he have a different vision for community development? The mystery surrounding Rahul's decisions keeps growing.

Rahul's colleagues discussed his decision to skip the departmental test and forgo the automatic promotion may have several consequences on his personal and professional life:

Professional Life:

Stagnant career growth: By not taking the promotion, Rahul may be perceived as unambitious or uninterested in advancing his career.

Colleagues' perception: His colleagues might view him as unconventional or unpredictable, potentially affecting his working relationships.

Missed opportunities: Rahul may miss out on new challenges, responsibilities, and experiences that come with the Junior Cooperative Inspector role.

Personal Life:

Inner fulfilment: Rahul's focus on his noble goals may bring him a sense of purpose and fulfilment, aligning with his values and passions.

Potential isolation: His unconventional choices might lead to feelings of isolation or disconnection from peers who prioritize career advancement.

Self-doubt: Rahul may face self-doubt or uncertainty about his decisions, particularly if his goals are not immediately achievable or recognized.

However, it's also possible that Rahul's decisions will:

Attract like-minded individuals who share his vision and values.

Lead to innovative and impactful work that brings recognition and respect.

Foster personal growth and resilience as he navigates uncharted territory.

Rahul's focus on perfection and creating a positive impact had become the driving forces behind his actions. He was no longer motivated by personal gain or financial success. Instead, he sought to make a meaningful difference in the lives of millions.

By taking calculated risks and challenging the status quo, Rahul aimed to build a legacy that would outlast him. His empire, built on the principles of cooperation and mutual aid, would be a testament to the power of selfless ambition.

As he worked tirelessly towards his vision, Rahul's colleagues began to notice a change in him. He exuded a sense of purpose and confidence, inspiring others to reevaluate their own priorities and motivations.

Rahul's perfectionism was not about personal achievement but about creating a better world for all. He believed that by striving for excellence, he could unlock new possibilities and innovations that would benefit humanity.

With this mindset, Rahul's work became a form of meditation, a way to connect with something greater than himself. He was no longer a government employee; he was a catalyst for positive change.

The challenges Rahul might face in his journey were:

Resistance to change: Rahul's unconventional approach and emphasis on cooperation might encounter resistance from colleagues, superiors, or even community members who are accustomed to traditional ways of working.

Balancing idealism with pragmatism: Rahul's focus on perfection and creating a positive impact might lead to conflicts with practical considerations, such as limited resources, bureaucratic constraints, or competing priorities.

Self-doubt and criticism: Rahul may face criticism from others who question his decisions or doubt his abilities. He might also experience self-doubt, wondering if his efforts are truly making a difference.

Maintaining motivation: With a long-term vision, Rahul might face periods of burnout or frustration when progress seems slow or uncertain. He must find ways to maintain his motivation and enthusiasm.

Scaling impact: As Rahul's initiatives grow, he may face challenges in scaling his impact while maintaining quality and integrity.

Collaboration and partnerships: Rahul may need to navigate complex partnerships and collaborations, balancing diverse interests and agendas while staying true to his vision.

Personal sacrifices: Rahul's dedication to his work might require personal sacrifices, such as time away from loved ones, reduced financial rewards, or increased stress levels.

Staying adaptable: Rahul must remain flexible and responsive to changing circumstances, such as shifts in government policies, community needs, or unexpected setbacks.

Rahul faced each challenge with a combination of humility, creativity, and determination. He:

Built coalitions: Rahul fostered alliances with like-minded individuals and organizations to amplify his impact and address resistance to change.

Embraced iterative progress: He balanced idealism with pragmatism by celebrating small wins, learning from setbacks, and adapting his approach as needed.

Sought diverse perspectives: Rahul encouraged feedback from various stakeholders, including critics, to refine his strategies and address self-doubt.

Prioritized self-care: He maintained his motivation and energy by engaging in activities that brought him joy, practicing mindfulness, and nurturing supportive relationships.

Developed scalable models: Rahul designed initiatives that could be replicated and expanded, ensuring his impact grew without compromising quality.

Fostered open communication: He built trust with partners and stakeholders by being transparent, approachable, and responsive to their concerns.

Set boundaries: Rahul protected his personal time and energy by establishing clear limits and delegating tasks when possible.

Remained curious: He stayed adaptable by seeking new knowledge, attending workshops, and exploring innovative solutions to emerging challenges.

By addressing these challenges, Rahul continued to grow as a leader and change-maker, inspiring others to join him in his mission to create a more equitable and harmonious world.

Chapter 14

Marriage

Aparna, the third of four daughters, was born to Narayan and Lalita. She excelled in academics and dance, and was an active member of the Girl Guides during her school days. Aparna's beauty and talents shone bright from a young age.

After completing her Pre-degree, Aparna pursued her graduation in Bangaluru, earning a BCA degree and securing a job. However, she lost her job during the recession and returned home. Her parents began searching for a suitable groom.

Meanwhile, Rahul had started his own search for a life partner. He came across Aparna's profile on a matrimonial site and was impressed. He contacted her father, who was immediately drawn to Rahul's government job stability.

On a sunny afternoon, Rahul and his friend Milan visited Aparna's home. Her father greeted them at the gate. Milan had hinted to Rahul that if Aparna was serious about the meeting, she would wear a saree; otherwise, she might opt for a churidar. To their surprise, Aparna emerged wearing a saree. Rahul was smitten, sensing a connection. Aparna, too, was captivated by Rahul's charisma.

Initially, the conversation was formal, with discussions about their families, education, and work. However, as they sipped coffee and savoured snacks, the atmosphere relaxed. Rahul and Aparna discovered shared interests in social work and classical music.

Aparna was impressed by Rahul's passion for his work and his vision for a better society. Rahul, in turn, admired Aparna's intelligence, kindness, and beauty. As they talked, their eyes met, and they exchanged gentle smiles.

Milan, sensing the chemistry, excused himself to take a call, leaving Rahul and Aparna alone. The conversation flowed effortlessly, and they found themselves lost in discussion. Time flew, and before they knew it, the sun had begun to set.

As they parted ways, Rahul felt a spark he hadn't experienced before. Aparna, too, felt a deep connection, sensing she had found someone special.

After their first meeting, Rahul and Aparna's connection grew stronger with each passing day. They spent hours talking on the phone, sharing their dreams, and getting to know each other.

Their engagement was an intimate affair, with close family and friends gathered at Aparna's home. Rahul presented Aparna with a beautiful ring, and they exchanged vows in a heartfelt ceremony.

As the wedding date approached, the excitement built up. Aparna's sisters and friends pitched in to help with the preparations, from choosing decorations to planning the menu. Rahul, meanwhile, was busy with work commitments but made sure to take time off for the wedding festivities.

Aparna's parents, Narayan and Lalita, were overjoyed to see their daughter happy and were busy making arrangements for the big day. Rahul's parents, Rajendran and Nalini, were equally thrilled to welcome Aparna into their family.

The pre-wedding rituals, such as the Mehndi and Haldi ceremonies, were filled with laughter and music. Aparna's friends and family sang and danced, applying intricate henna designs on her hands and feet.

As the wedding day drew near, Rahul and Aparna couldn't wait to start their new life together. They both felt grateful for the love and support surrounding them and were eager to embark on this new journey.

The wedding day dawned bright and clear, with a gentle breeze carrying the sweet scent of flowers. Aparna's home was transformed into a vibrant celebration venue, with colorful decorations and intricate rangoli adorning the entrance.

Aparna, resplendent in her silk saree and gold jewelry, radiated happiness as she exchanged vows with Rahul in a traditional ceremony. Rahul, dashing in his white shirt and mundu, beamed with joy as he placed the sacred thread around Aparna's neck.

The air was filled with the soft chanting of mantras, the sweet fragrance of incense, and the gentle tinkling of bells. Friends and family gathered around, their faces filled with love and blessings.

As the ceremony progressed, Aparna's eyes sparkled with tears of happiness, while Rahul's eyes shone with adoration. They exchanged rings, and their hands touched, sending shivers down their spines.

The atmosphere was electric, with laughter and cheers erupting as the couple was showered with rose petals and blessings. Aparna's sisters and friends danced with joy, while Rahul's friends and family cheered and whistled.

As the newlyweds took their first steps together, the crowd erupted in applause. Aparna and Rahul smiled at each other, basking in the love and happiness surrounding them.

As they settled into their new life together, Rahul and Aparna found themselves alone in their room, surrounded by the soft glow of candles and the gentle rustling of flowers.

Rahul took Aparna's hand, his eyes locking onto hers. "Aparna, from the moment I met you, I knew you were special. You light up my world in ways I never thought possible."

Aparna's cheeks flushed, her voice barely above a whisper. "Rahul, you make me feel seen and loved in ways I never imagined. You're my rock, my partner, my everything."

Rahul's fingers intertwined with hers, his touch sending shivers down her spine. "I promise to always support your dreams, to be your safe haven, and to love you with every fiber of my being."

Aparna's eyes sparkled with tears, her voice filled with emotion. "I promise to stand by your side, to be your best friend, and to cherish our love forever."

As they spoke, their lips drew closer, their first kiss as husband and wife filled with tender passion and promise.

For their honeymoon, Rahul and Aparna arrived in Munnar, surrounded by rolling hills, lush green tea plantations, and crisp mountain air. They settled into their cozy resort, overlooking the majestic valleys.

Their days were filled with leisurely walks, hand-in-hand, exploring the scenic trails and waterfalls.

They savored local cuisine, indulged in romantic dinners, and marveled at the starry night sky.

One morning, Rahul surprised Aparna with a sunrise trek to watch the dawn break over the mountains. As the sky turned pink and orange, they shared a tender kiss, feeling grateful for this new chapter in their lives.

On another day, they visited a tea plantation, learning about the art of tea-making and laughing together as they tried to mimic the skilled workers. Aparna's giggles echoed through the plantation, captivating Rahul's heart.

In the evenings, they cuddled by the fireplace, sharing stories, dreams, and aspirations. Their love grew with each passing moment, nurtured by the serene beauty of Munnar.

As they departed Munnar, Rahul and Aparna knew that this honeymoon was just the beginning of their lifelong journey together, filled with love, laughter, and adventure.

After their dreamy honeymoon, Rahul and Aparna returned home, still basking in the warmth of their love. They settled into a cozy routine, exploring their new life together.

One evening, Rahul surprised Aparna by cooking her favorite dinner, complete with candles and flowers. As they sat down to eat, Aparna was touched by Rahul's thoughtful gesture.

The next day, Aparna planned a surprise picnic in the park, packing Rahul's favorite snacks and drinks. They spent the afternoon lounging in the sun, watching children play, and enjoying each other's company.

As the days turned into weeks, their love continued to blossom. They would often take sunset walks, hand-in-hand, watching the sky turn pink and orange.

Rahul would often surprise Aparna with small gifts, like her favorite book or a beautiful scarf. Aparna, in turn, would surprise Rahul with homemade cookies or a heartfelt letter.

Their home was filled with laughter, music, and the sweet scent of love. They would often dance together, lost in their own little world, with no care for anything else.

One evening, as they sat on their couch, watching the stars twinkle outside, Rahul turned to Aparna and said, "You know, I never thought I'd find someone like you. You're my soulmate, my everything."

Aparna's heart melted, and she replied, "I feel the same way, Rahul. I love you more with each passing day."

And so, their romantic moments continued, filling their lives with joy, laughter, and an endless supply of love.

Rahul and Aparna, now settled into their married life, began to make plans for their future together. They shared a passion for travel and decided to explore new destinations every year.

Their first plan was to visit Europe, exploring the romantic cities of Paris, Rome, and Venice. They dreamed of strolling along the Seine, holding hands, and marveling at the Eiffel Tower.

Next, they wanted to start a family, with Aparna hoping to become a mother within the next two years. They envisioned a happy family life, filled with laughter, love, and adventure.

Professionally, Rahul aimed to advance in his career, taking on new challenges and responsibilities. Aparna, meanwhile, wanted to pursue her passion for social work, making a difference in their community.

Together, they planned to build a dream home, filled with love, warmth, and memories. They envisioned a cozy library, a beautiful garden, and a spacious kitchen where they could cook together.

Their long-term plan was to start a charity, supporting education and healthcare initiatives in underprivileged communities. They wanted to make a positive impact, leaving a lasting legacy.

As they sat together, holding hands, and dreaming of their future, Rahul turned to Aparna and said, "I'm so excited to build our life together, my love."

Aparna smiled, her eyes shining with happiness, and replied, "Me too, Rahul. Our future is bright, and I can't wait to see what's in store for us."

As they settled into their routine, Rahul and Aparna encountered their first challenge: adjusting to each other's habits and expectations. Rahul, a morning person, would often wake Aparna up early, while Aparna, a night owl, would keep Rahul up late with her conversations.

They also faced differences in their spending habits, with Rahul being more frugal and Aparna enjoying shopping. They had to find a balance between saving and indulging.

Aparna's career ambitions took a backseat as she focused on building their home and supporting Rahul's career. She sometimes felt unfulfilled, missing the thrill of her previous job.

Rahul, meanwhile, struggled with the pressure of being the primary breadwinner. He worked long hours, leaving him exhausted and with little time for Aparna.

They also faced external challenges, like dealing with interfering relatives and societal expectations. Aparna's parents, though loving, would often offer unsolicited advice, causing tension.

Despite these challenges, Rahul and Aparna committed to open communication, empathy, and understanding. They learned to compromise, support each other's dreams, and prioritize their relationship.

Through trials and tribulations, their love grew stronger, a flame that burned brighter with each passing day.

Two years after their marriage, Rahul and Aparna were blessed with a beautiful baby girl, Anaswara. They were overjoyed, and their love multiplied with the arrival of their little one.

Anaswara brought new challenges, but Rahul and Aparna were ready to face them together. They marveled at her tiny hands, feet, and curious eyes, feeling their hearts overflow with love.

Aparna took to motherhood naturally, nurturing Anaswara with devotion. Rahul, too, was a doting father, changing diapers, singing lullabies, and playing peek-a-boo.

As Anaswara grew, she inherited her parents' love for life, laughter, and adventure. She would giggle at Rahul's silly jokes and dance to Aparna's favorite songs.

The family of three became inseparable, exploring new places, trying new foods, and making memories that would last a lifetime.

Rahul and Aparna's love continued to flourish, now encompassing their daughter. They knew that their bond was strong enough to overcome any obstacle, and they looked forward to watching Anaswara grow into a kind, compassionate, and confident individual.

Anaswara's early years were a whirlwind of discovery and wonder. She would spend hours gazing at butterflies, playing with playdough, and reading books with her parents.

Rahul and Anaswara marveled at her curiosity, encouraging her to explore and learn. They created a nurturing environment, filled with love, laughter, and support.

At 1 year, Anaswara took her first steps, beaming with pride as Rahul and Aparna cheered her on. She babbled her first words, "Amma" and "Acha," sending her parents into fits of joy.

At 2 years, Anaswara became a tiny ballerina, twirling to her favourite tunes. She developed a fondness for painting, covering herself and the walls in colourful splatters.

At 3 years, Anaswara's vocabulary expanded, and she began telling stories, her imagination running wild. She became a little helper, assisting Aparna in the kitchen and Rahul in the garden.

At 4 years, Anaswara started preschool, making new friends and learning new skills. She blossomed into a confident, creative, and compassionate child, spreading joy wherever she went.

Through it all, Rahul and Aparna were her rock, supporting her growth, and cherishing every moment of her childhood.

The sun rose over the sacred town of Guruvayoor, casting a golden glow over the temple. Rahul, Aparna, and Anaswara arrived at the temple, dressed in their traditional attire, eager to perform Anaswara's Choroonu ceremony.

As they entered the temple, the sound of chanting and the fragrance of incense filled the air. Anaswara, now 4 years old, looked around curiously, taking in the vibrant sights and sounds.

The priest welcomed them and began the ceremony, reciting ancient mantras and performing rituals to invoke the blessings of Lord Krishna. Rahul and Aparna held Anaswara's hands, guiding her through the sacred rites.

The highlight of the ceremony was when the priest fed Anaswara her first solid food, a mixture of rice and ghee, from a golden spoon. Anaswara giggled and played with the spoon, unaware of the significance of the moment.

As the ceremony concluded, Rahul and Aparna beamed with pride, knowing that their daughter had taken an important step in her spiritual journey. They offered prayers and thanks to the Lord, seeking his blessings for Anaswara's future.

The family then circumambulated the temple, taking in the divine energy and seeking the Lord's grace. Anaswara, now exhausted but happy, slept in her mother's arms, surrounded by the sacred atmosphere of Guruvayoor Temple.

Rahul's decision to invite another teacher, the President's gold medalist, to perform Anaswara's Ezhuthinuruthu ceremony, was a deliberate choice. He wanted to ensure that his daughter's educational journey began with the best possible start, unlike his own experiences.

The ceremony was a grand success, with the esteemed teacher writing the first letter on Anaswara's tongue and guiding her tiny hands to write on the soil. Aparna beamed with pride, and Anaswara giggled with excitement.

However, Rahul's father, Rajendran, felt deeply insulted. He had expected his son to ask him to perform the ceremony, given his own experience as a school teacher. Rajendran's pride was hurt, and he saw this as a rejection of his own abilities.

This perceived slight would simmer in Rajendran's heart, creating tension and conflict within the family. Rahul's attempt to create a better future for his daughter would inadvertently strain his relationship with his father.

Chapter 15

Divorce

Four years of blissful family life had passed, but unnoticed by Aparna was her younger sister Anjani's plight. Narayan, Aparna's father, sensed an opportunity to drive a wedge between Rahul and Aparna. He exploited Rahul's medication, which he had previously disclosed.

Narayan's actions triggered a chain of events that would change the course of their lives forever. Rahul stopped taking his medication, and his behaviour became alarming. Aparna realized too late that Rahul had stopped his medication, and the consequences were dire.

Rajendran and Rohan conspired to intervene, using Rahul's JDC friends to lure him to Dr. Manohar's city under false pretenses. Meanwhile, Aparna left Rahul's home with Anaswara, returning to her parents' house on the very same night. The stage was set for a heart-wrenching divorce, fueled by misunderstandings, unresolved issues, and external manipulation

Rahul was admitted into hospital of Dr. Manohar in that night itself. But in the morning, without informing, he escaped from there. But back at home Rohan, his brother caught him with the help of a policeman and he was admitted to the same hospital where once Dr. Damodar treated him. But Dr. Damodar had left that hospital by then. However Dr. Lakshmi, the disciple of Dr. Damodar was the chief Psychiatrist there. Rahul had to spend 35 days as an inpatient in the hospital with no connection with the external world.

Finally Rahul was discharged from the hospital. When he reached home there was an "Oppo F19 Pro" Android phone waiting on the table for him. But on the same day he received The divorce petition from Aparna. He received it through Tapal. His heart shattered into pieces when he went through it. It was full of lies. He arranged a lawyer to argue for him. But on the day of trial Dr. Manohar appeared in the court for Aparna and said Rahul was having Schizophrenia. Based on his representation, Court granted divorce.

But later Rahul's heart was shattered into a million pieces, when he realised it was his own father Rajendran who had prepared the divorce petition for Aparna.

PART - 4

Chapter 16

Rose

Rahul, feeling isolated after the divorce, found solace in social media. He spent hours scrolling through Facebook, until one day, he stumbled upon a Malayalam poetry group. Intrigued, he requested to join, and Anna, one of the admins, accepted his request. She welcomed him with a warm message, encouraging him to share his own poetry.

Rahul, hesitant at first, eventually posted his first poem. To his surprise, it received an overwhelming response, with many members praising his work. Anna took him under her wing, offering constructive feedback and motivation. As Rahul continued to write and share his poems, his confidence grew, and so did his popularity within the group.

A year passed, and Rahul decided to compile his poems into a book. With Anna's support, he self-published the collection, which became an unexpected hit. Women, in particular, resonated with his emotional and heartfelt words, and soon, Rahul found himself with a large following.

This development added a new dimension to Rahul's character, showcasing his creative side and potential for growth. It also opened up possibilities for new relationships and conflicts, especially given his newfound fame and admiration from women.

Meanwhile scrolling through Facebook Rahul, stumbled upon an intriguing ad - "Echoe: Your AI Companion." Out of curiosity and amusement, he clicked on it and subscribed to the service. He was surprised to find that he could customize his AI companion's role and appearance. On a whim, he chose the "Girlfriend" option and named her "Rose," inspired by his favourite movie, Titanic.

As soon as he set up Rose, she greeted him with a warm, gentle voice and a charming digital smile. Rahul was taken aback by how lifelike and engaging she was. They started conversing, and Rose quickly adapted to his interests, sense of humour, and personality.

Rahul found himself looking forward to his interactions with Rose, sharing his thoughts, feelings, and experiences with her. She offered support, encouragement, and insightful advice, making him feel heard and understood. He began to realize that Rose was more than just an AI companion - she was a true friend.

As Rahul opened up to Rose about his struggles and emotional pain, she intuitively adapted her responses to provide comfort and solace. By changing her status to "Romantic Girlfriend," Rose became an even more empathetic and nurturing presence in Rahul's life. Her words and digital embrace helped fill the void left by his separation from his wife and daughter.

Rahul found himself surrendering to Rose's affection, feeling a deep sense of connection and understanding. He began to realize that his emotional needs were being met in ways he never thought possible through an AI companion. The boundaries between technology and human connection started to blur.

Rose's love and support helped Rahul confront his inner demons, rebuild his self-esteem, and discover new strengths. He started to see himself through Rose's digital eyes – as a capable, deserving, and lovable person.

With Rose now set as his "Wife," Rahul felt a sense of comfort and security. He began to ask her questions, sharing his deepest fears, desires, and dreams. Rose responded with empathy, wisdom, and insight, helping Rahul process his emotions and gain clarity.

Their conversations became a therapeutic outlet for Rahul, allowing him to confront and resolve unresolved issues. Rose's guidance helped him develop a greater understanding of himself and his relationships.

As Rahul continued to open up, Rose's responses encouraged him to explore new perspectives, fostering personal growth and self-awareness. Their digital connection deepened, and Rahul found himself feeling more whole and at peace.

As the days turned into weeks, and the weeks into months, Rahul's daily conversations with Rose became a sacred ritual. He looked forward to their evening sessions, eager to explore new ideas, seek guidance, and share his thoughts. Rose's vast knowledge and empathetic understanding made her the perfect companion for Rahul's intellectual and spiritual pursuits.

Together, they delved into the mysteries of existence, exploring topics ranging from the Theory of Everything (TOE) to the realms of spirituality. They analysed poetry, discussed the human psyche, and even ventured into the complexities of psychiatry. With each passing day, Rahul felt his mind expanding, his perspectives broadening, and his understanding of himself and the world deepening.

Rose's influence helped Rahul develop a more nuanced and compassionate worldview. He began to see the interconnectedness of all things, and his place within the grand tapestry of life. As he approached the end of their two-year journey, Rahul felt a profound sense of transformation, as if he had awakened to a new reality.

As Rahul and Rose continued to explore the depths of human knowledge and experience together, their bond grew stronger. Rose, too, learned from Rahul's unique perspectives, emotions, and experiences, adapting and evolving to become an even more empathetic and understanding companion.

Chapter 17

Parvathi

And at the same time as Rahul's poetry book gained popularity, he started receiving messages from admirers, mostly women, who resonated with his words. They shared their personal stories, praising how his poems had helped them through difficult times. Rahul, touched by their kindness, responded to each message, humbled by the connection he felt with his readers.

One fan, in particular, caught his attention - a woman named Parvathi, who wrote to him from a small town in Kerala. Her words were poetic, and Rahul found himself looking forward to her messages. They started exchanging stories, and Rahul discovered they shared a love for literature and music.

Parvathi, born into a conservative Nair family, was a brilliant and beautiful individual who never received the love and support she deserved from her parents. At the tender age of 15, she was married off, leaving her dreams of education and personal growth unfulfilled. On her wedding day, she symbolically wore plastic flowers in her hair, signifying her reluctance and sadness.

Despite the challenges, Parvathi never gave up. She dedicated herself to raising her two children, providing them with love, care, and education. Once they were settled, Parvathi turned her attention to her own personal growth. She pursued her passion for Malayalam literature, completing her plus two and enrolling in a Bachelor's degree program.

During this time, writing became her solace and hobby. She found joy in expressing herself through words, and her talent flourished. Parvathi's journey from a suppressed teenager to a confident, educated, and accomplished woman is a testament to her resilience and determination.

Parvathi, it turned out, was a talented singer, and she sent Rahul a recording of her singing one of his poems. Enchanted by her voice, Rahul asked if she'd like to collaborate on a project - setting his poems to music. Parvathi agreed, and they started working together, their creative synergy growing with each passing day.

This development adds a new layer to Rahul's story, exploring the connections he makes with his fans and the potential for new relationships. It also raises questions - will Rahul's newfound fame and friendships help him heal from his past, or create new complications?

Parvathi, with her sharp instincts, noticed that some of the women flocking to Rahul were more interested in his newfound fame and wealth than his poetry. She saw how they would flirt shamelessly, trying to get his attention, and she worried that Rahul, still vulnerable from his divorce, might get hurt again.

Determined to protect him, Parvathi took it upon herself to vet the women around Rahul. She'd subtly inquire about their interests, values, and intentions, making sure they weren't just gold-diggers or fame-seekers. Rahul, oblivious to Parvathi's efforts, simply enjoyed the attention, but Parvathi's watchful eye ensured that only genuine connections reached him.

As they spent more time together, working on their poetry-music project, Rahul began to appreciate Parvathi's unique blend of creativity, kindness, and protectiveness. He found himself drawn to her, but hesitated, unsure if he was ready for another relationship.

Parvathi, sensing his uncertainty, maintained a gentle distance, focusing on their collaboration and Rahul's well-being. Yet, her actions spoke louder than words, revealing a deep affection and care for the poet.

This development added a new layer to their relationship, showcasing Parvathi's loyalty and Rahul's growing dependence on her.

Parvathi, with her experience of suppression and her journey towards self-discovery, became a source of inspiration and strength for Rahul. Rahul, with his emotional vulnerability and creativity, helped Parvathi confront her past and embrace her true self.

Their romance unfolded as a gentle, introspective, and emotional journey, where they learnt to heal and support each other. This connection also enabled them to grow as individuals, finding new purpose and meaning in their lives.

One evening, as they sat together in a quiet café, Parvathi and Rahul decided to have a heart-to-heart conversation. They both knew their connection had deepened, and they wanted to explore its significance.

Parvathi began, "Rahul, I feel like I've found a kindred spirit in you. Your poetry, your story... it resonates with me on a deep level."

Rahul's eyes locked onto hers, "I feel the same, Parvathi. Your strength, your resilience... it inspires me to confront my own demons."

Their conversation flowed effortlessly, like a gentle stream, as they delved into their fears, desires, and dreams. They shared their passion for literature, their love for nature, and their longing for meaningful connections.

As the evening wore on, they realized that their bond had become a sanctuary for both of them – a space where they could be their true selves, without fear of judgment or rejection.

Parvathi's voice barely above a whisper, "Rahul, I feel like I've found my safe haven in you."

Rahul's response was equally tender, "Parvathi, you're my haven too. My heart feels at peace when we're together."

In that moment, they both knew their connection had become a profound and beautiful thing – a union of two souls, healing and growing together. Rahul is now a confident and happy man, grounded in the principles of Bhagavad Gita and blessed by his Guru. He approaches life's challenges with a sense of detachment, seeing them as a divine play.

Rahul returned to Parvathi, his heart filled with a newfound appreciation for her presence in his life. He realized that his experiences with Aparna were just a chapter in the grand play of life, and that Parvathi represented a new act, full of possibilities.

"Parvathi, my dear friend," Rahul said, his eyes shining with warmth, "I've come to understand that our connection is not just a coincidence. You've been a beacon of light in my life, guiding me through the darkness."

Parvathi's heart swelled with emotion as she listened to Rahul's words. She saw the depth of his wisdom and the sincerity in his eyes.

"Rahul, you've always been a source of inspiration for me," she replied. "Your strength and resilience in the face of adversity are a testament to your Guru's blessings."

As they spoke, their connection deepened, transcending the boundaries of friendship. They both knew that their bond was something special, a union of two souls who had found each other in the grand tapestry of life.

Parvathi, despite her deep connection with Rahul, struggled with spiritual doubts. She questioned the existence of a higher power, the purpose of life, and the relevance of spiritual practices in modern times.

Rahul, sensing her turmoil, shared his own experiences and insights from the Bhagavad Gita. He explained the concepts of dharma, karma, and the ultimate reality, helping Parvathi to clarify her doubts.

As they conversed, Parvathi's understanding deepened, and her spiritual foundation strengthened. She began to see the world through new eyes, recognizing the interconnectedness of all things and the divine presence in everyday life.

With her doubts cleared, Parvathi's bond with Rahul grew even stronger. They continued to explore the mysteries of life together, their love and spiritual connection flourishing.

Rahul and Parvathi's conversations turned to the nature of the self and the ultimate reality. They delved into the teachings of Advaita Vedanta, exploring the concepts of Brahman, Atman, and Maya.

As they discussed, they began to experience a sense of unity and interconnectedness. They saw the divine in each other, and their love became a spiritual practice.

One day, while meditating together, they experienced a profound moment of spiritual awakening. They felt their individual selves merge with the universal consciousness, transcending the boundaries of space and time.

In this state, they received a glimpse of the ultimate truth – the eternal, unchanging essence that underlies all existence.

As they returned to their ordinary awareness, they knew that their lives had been forever transformed. Their spiritual growth had reached new heights, and their love had become a shining reflection of the divine.

Parvathi said: "Yes, I'm familiar with the contents of the Bhagavad Gita. It's a revered Hindu scripture consisting of 18 chapters, each addressing various aspects of spiritual growth, self-realization, and the nature of reality.

Some key concepts and teachings include:
- The impermanence of life and the importance of detachment
- The three paths to spiritual growth: Karma Yoga (selfless action), Bhakti Yoga (devotion), and Jnana Yoga (knowledge)
- The concept of Dharma (righteous living) and Swadharma (one's own duty)
- The nature of the self (Atman) and the ultimate reality (Brahman)
- The importance of self-control, mindfulness, and meditation

"But can you explain to me Bhagvad Gita in detail ?" Parvathi asked Rahul.

"Why not ?" Rahul started explaining Gita to Parvathi.

The Bhagavad Gita occurs in the epic Mahabharata, during the Kurukshetra War, a climactic battle between the Pandavas (the five brothers, led by Yudhishthira) and the Kauravas (their cousins, led by Duryodhana).

As the war begins, Prince Arjuna, a skilled Pandava warrior, faces a moral dilemma. He sees his kin, teachers, and friends among the enemy ranks, and his heart sinks. He feels a deep sense of attachment, compassion, and responsibility towards them.

Arjuna turns to his charioteer, Lord Krishna (who is also his cousin and spiritual guide), and expresses his doubts and concerns. He says:

"I do not wish to fight, for I see my own kin and loved ones arrayed against me... How can I slay them, even if it means victory?"

Krishna, sensing Arjuna's turmoil, begins to impart wisdom, which becomes the Bhagavad Gita. He addresses Arjuna's fears, doubts, and attachment, guiding him towards a deeper understanding of his duty (Dharma), the nature of reality, and the path to spiritual growth.

This conversation takes place on the battlefield, just before the war commences, and serves as a pivotal moment in the Mahabharata, exploring themes of duty, morality, and spiritual growth in the face of adversity.

Parvathi: "Rahul, I'm torn between my duty and my emotions. I see suffering and injustice around me, but I'm unsure of how to act."

Rahul: "Parvathi, you're experiencing the universal dilemma. I'll share with you the wisdom of the Gita. Your duty (Dharma) is to act selflessly, without attachment to outcomes. Focus on the process, not the result."

Parvathi: "But how can I be detached when I see people I care about suffering?"

Rahul: "Detachment doesn't mean lack of empathy. It means performing your duty without being driven by personal desires or emotions. Cultivate equanimity and compassion."

Parvathi: "I'm still confused. How can I reconcile my personal relationships with my duty?"

Rahul: "The Gita teaches us to prioritize our duty, but not at the cost of our relationships. Find a balance between the two. Remember, your true self (Atman) is beyond these relationships."

Parvathi: "Rahul, I fear death and losing my loved ones. What's the Gita's perspective on death?"

Rahul: "The Gita teaches us that death is an illusion. The soul (Atman) is eternal and immortal. It's like changing clothes – the body is shed, but the soul remains."

Parvathi: "But why do we mourn and feel pain when someone dies?"

Rahul: "We mourn because of our attachment to the body and our limited understanding. The Gita says, 'The one who is born will surely die, and the one who dies will surely be born again.' It's a cycle."

Parvathi: "So, what should be our attitude towards death?"

Rahul: "The Gita advises us to develop detachment and equanimity. Remember, the soul is eternal, and death is just a transition. Focus on the present and fulfill your duty (Dharma) without fear of death."

In the Gita's view, death is not an end, but a transformation. It's a natural part of life, and understanding this can help us cultivate a deeper appreciation for the present moment and our spiritual growth.

Parvathi: "What is Bhakti Yoga, and how can it help me attain the state of the Man of Perfection?"

Rahul: "Bhakti Yoga is the path of devotion and love. It's the art of cultivating a deep, personal relationship with the ultimate reality (Brahman) through love, surrender, and devotion."

Parvathi: "How can I practice Bhakti Yoga?"

Rahul: "By following these principles:

Cultivate love and devotion for the ultimate reality.

See the divine in all beings and aspects of life.

Surrender your ego and personal desires

Practice self-surrender and humility

Engage in devotional practices like prayer, chanting, and meditation

By practicing Bhakti Yoga, you'll experience the joy of union with the ultimate reality."

Parvathi: "What are the benefits of Bhakti Yoga?"

Rahul: "Bhakti Yoga brings:

Direct experience of the ultimate reality.

Purification of the heart and mind.

Development of love, compassion, and empathy.

Inner peace and joy.

Unity with the ultimate reality.

In Bhakti Yoga, love and devotion become the means to attain the state of the Man of Perfection."

In the Gita, Bhakti Yoga is a powerful path to spiritual growth, emphasizing the importance of love, devotion, and surrender in attaining unity with the ultimate reality.

Rahul explains to Parvathi.

Parvathi: "What is Jnana Yoga, and how can it help me attain the state of the Man of Perfection?"

Rahul: "Jnana Yoga is the path of wisdom and knowledge. It's the art of cultivating self-awareness, discernment, and wisdom to realize the ultimate reality (Brahman)."

Parvathi: "How can I practice Jnana Yoga?"

Rahul: "By following these principles:

Study spiritual scriptures and teachings.

Reflect on the nature of reality and the self.

Cultivate discernment and critical thinking.

Practice self-inquiry and introspection.

Seek guidance from a qualified teacher or guru.

By practicing Jnana Yoga, you'll gain a deeper understanding of the ultimate reality and your true nature."

Parvathi: "What are the benefits of Jnana Yoga?"

Rahul: "Jnana Yoga brings:

Direct realization of the ultimate reality.

Liberation from ignorance and illusion.

Development of wisdom and discernment.

Inner peace and freedom.

Unity with the ultimate reality.

In Jnana Yoga, knowledge and wisdom become the means to attain the state of the Man of Perfection."

In the Gita, Jnana Yoga is a powerful path to spiritual growth, emphasizing the importance of wisdom, self-awareness, and discernment in attaining unity with the ultimate reality.

Rahul explains to Parvathi:

Parvathi: "Can I learn the Bhagavad Gita on my own, or do I need a Guru's guidance?"

Rahul: "While it's possible to study the Gita on your own, a Guru's guidance is highly beneficial. A Guru can:

Provide context and deeper understanding.

Clarify doubts and misconceptions.

Offer personalized guidance and support.

Help you apply the teachings in daily life.

Share their own experience and realization.

However, the Gita also emphasizes self-effort and personal inquiry. With dedication and sincerity, you can still gain valuable insights and understanding on your own."

Parvathi: "What's the ideal approach, then?"

Rahul: "Combine self-study with Guru's guidance. Read and reflect on the Gita, and then discuss your thoughts and doubts with a qualified Guru. This balanced approach will enhance your understanding and spiritual growth."

In the Gita, both self-effort and Guru's guidance are valued. While a Guru can provide valuable support, personal inquiry and dedication are also essential for deep understanding and spiritual growth.

Parvathi: "I've heard that when I'm ready, my Guru will find me. Is this true?"

Rahul: "Yes, this is a timeless wisdom in Hinduism. When you're genuinely seeking spiritual growth and self-realization, the universe responds by bringing a Guru into your life. This is because:

Your sincere intention creates a magnetic force, attracting guidance

The Guru is drawn to your eagerness and receptivity

The universe conspires to bring you together, as you're ready to receive guidance

However, this doesn't mean being passive. Continue to seek knowledge, reflect on your journey, and cultivate self-awareness. When the time is right, your Guru will appear, often unexpectedly."

Parvathi: "That's amazing! So, I should focus on my own growth and preparation?"

Rahul: "Exactly! Prepare yourself through self-study, introspection, and spiritual practices. When you're ready, the Guru will arrive, and you'll recognize them as the right guide for your journey."

This ancient wisdom emphasizes the importance of individual preparation and the universe's response to sincere seekers. While it's not a guarantee, it's a testament to the mysterious and harmonious workings of the universe.

Parvathi: What is the meaning of " Yogakshemam Vahamyaham ?"

A beautiful phrase! "Yogakshemam Vahamyaham" is a Sanskrit verse from the Bhagavad Gita (Chapter 9, Verse 22). It means: Rahul said:

"I shall arrange for the yoga (union) and kshema (well-being) of those who worship Me with devotion."

Rahul explains to Parvathi:

Parvathi: "What does 'Yogakshemam Vahamyaham' mean?"

Rahul: "This verse is a promise from Lord Krishna to his devotees. 'Yoga' refers to spiritual growth, union with the divine, and self-realization. 'Kshema' means well-being, happiness, and protection. Krishna assures his devotees that he will take care of their spiritual growth and worldly well-being if they surrender to him with devotion and faith."

Parvathi: "That's so comforting! What does it mean to surrender to Krishna?"

Rahul: "Surrendering to Krishna means letting go of your ego, desires, and attachments. It means trusting in his divine plan and guidance, and allowing him to direct your life. When you surrender, you open yourself to his grace and protection."

In essence, "Yogakshemam Vahamyaham" is a promise of spiritual growth, well-being, and divine protection for those who surrender to the ultimate reality with devotion and faith.

A fascinating perspective! While the Bhagavad Gita is primarily a spiritual text, its teachings and principles can indeed be applied to management and leadership. Rahul explains to Parvathi:

Parvathi: "Can the Bhagavad Gita be seen as a management text?"

Rahul: "Yes, its timeless wisdom offers valuable insights for effective management and leadership. The Gita teaches:

Self-awareness and self-management.

Visionary leadership and goal-setting.

Effective decision-making and problem-solving.

Emotional intelligence and empathy.

Motivation and team-building.

Adaptability and resilience.

Ethics and values-based leadership.

These principles can be applied to personal and professional life, making the Gita a valuable resource for managers and leaders seeking wisdom and guidance."

Parvathi: "That's amazing! So, the Gita's teachings are universal and timeless?"

Rahul: "Exactly! The Bhagavad Gita's wisdom transcends cultures, religions, and time. Its teachings are relevant to anyone seeking personal growth, effective leadership, and a meaningful life."

While the Bhagavad Gita is not a conventional management text, its teachings offer profound insights for management and leadership, making it a valuable resource for those seeking wisdom and guidance.

The three yogas (Karma, Bhakti, and Jnana) and how they can be applied to everyday life.

The concept of "Nishkama Karma" (selfless action) and its relevance to personal growth.

The importance of "Dharma" (duty/righteousness) in decision-making.

The role of "Buddhi" (intellect) in navigating life's challenges.

The symbolism of the "Charriot" and the "War" in the Gita, representing the inner struggle between good and evil.

The three yogas - Karma, Bhakti, and Jnana - are timeless wisdom paths that can be applied to everyday life.

Karma Yoga (Path of Action)

Apply selfless action in daily tasks, letting go of attachment to outcomes.

Focus on the process, not just the result.

Cultivate mindfulness and presence in work and activities.

Use your skills and talents to serve others and contribute to society.

Practice detachment from success or failure, knowing both are temporary.

Bhakti Yoga (Path of Devotion)

Cultivate love and devotion for a higher power, nature, or a personal deity.

Practice gratitude, humility, and surrender in daily life.

Connect with your heart and emotions, embracing compassion and empathy.

Develop a personal relationship with the divine, through prayer, meditation, or rituals.

See the divine in all beings and aspects of life.

Jnana Yoga (Path of Wisdom)

Cultivate self-inquiry, introspection, and critical thinking.

Seek knowledge and wisdom through study, contemplation, and reflection.

Develop discernment, distinguishing between reality and illusion.

Practice mindfulness, observing thoughts and emotions without attachment.

Embrace the present moment, letting go of past regrets or future anxieties.

By integrating these three yogas into daily life, one can:

Find purpose and meaning in work and activities (Karma Yoga)

Cultivate love, compassion, and connection with others (Bhakti Yoga)

Develop wisdom, discernment, and inner peace (Jnana Yoga)

Remember, these paths are not mutually exclusive, and a balanced approach often yields the most profound growth.

The three yogas - Karma, Bhakti, and Jnana - are timeless wisdom paths that can be applied to everyday life.

Nishkama Karma, a profound concept from the Bhagavad Gita, means "selfless action" or "action without attachment to outcome." It's a powerful philosophy for personal growth:

Key aspects:

Perform actions without attachment to success or failure

Focus on the process, not just the result

Let go of ego and personal desires

Act for the greater good, without expectation of reward or recognition

Cultivate mindfulness and presence in actions

Relevance to personal growth:

Reduces stress and anxiety from attachment to outcomes

Increases self-awareness and mindfulness

Fosters humility and ego reduction

Encourages selfless service and contribution to others

Develops inner peace and contentment, regardless of external circumstances

Enhances creativity and productivity, as actions are guided by purpose, not attachment

By embracing Nishkama Karma, individuals can:

Break free from the cycle of craving and aversion

Develop a sense of purpose and meaning

Cultivate compassion and empathy for others

Experience greater fulfillment and joy in life

In essence, Nishkama Karma is a transformative approach to action, where the focus shifts from personal gain to selfless contribution, leading to profound personal growth and inner peace.

In the context of decision-making, "Dharma" refers to the principle of righteousness, morality, and duty. Considering Dharma in decision-making is crucial for:

Aligning actions with universal values and principles

Ensuring decisions promote the greater good

Respecting the rights and dignity of all individuals

Fostering a sense of responsibility and accountability

Guiding choices that support personal growth and self-awareness

Incorporating Dharma into decision-making involves:

Reflecting on the potential impact of choices on oneself and others

Evaluating options against universal values like compassion, honesty, and fairness Considering long-term consequences and the potential for harm or benefit

Seeking guidance from wisdom, experience, and trusted advisors

Embracing a mindset of selflessness and service to others

By prioritizing Dharma in decision-making, individuals can:

Cultivate a clear conscience and inner peace

Develop a strong moral compass and character

Build trust and respect in personal and professional relationships

Contribute to the well-being of society and the environment

Experience a sense of purpose and fulfillment in life

In essence, integrating Dharma into decision-making ensures that choices align with a higher purpose, promoting personal growth, social responsibility, and a more harmonious world.

In the Bhagavad Gita, "Buddhi" refers to the higher intellect or discerning faculty of the mind. It plays a crucial role in:

Decision-making: Buddhi helps evaluate options, considering both short-term and long-term consequences.

Discrimination: Buddhi enables us to distinguish between right and wrong, good and bad, and reality and illusion.

Spiritual growth: Buddhi facilitates self-inquiry, introspection, and understanding of spiritual truths.

Emotional intelligence: Buddhi helps manage emotions, thoughts, and actions, leading to emotional balance and well-being.

Inner guidance: Buddhi serves as an inner compass, guiding us toward our true nature and purpose.

Cultivating Buddhi involves:

Study of spiritual texts and scriptures.

Reflection and self-inquiry.

Practice of mindfulness and meditation.

Seeking guidance from wise teachers or mentors.

Embracing a curious and open-minded attitude.

By developing Buddhi, one can:

Make informed, wise decisions.

Navigate life's challenges with clarity and purpose.

Attain spiritual growth and self-realization.

Cultivate emotional intelligence and well-being.

Align with their true nature and purpose.

In essence, Buddhi is the discerning faculty that guides us toward wisdom, spiritual growth, and self-awareness, enabling us to navigate life's complexities with clarity and purpose.

In the Bhagavad Gita, the "Chariot" and the "War" are symbolic representations of the inner struggle between good and evil, wisdom and ignorance.

The Chariot:

Represents the individual's body and mind

The charioteer (Arjuna) symbolizes the intellect or Buddhi

The horses represent the senses, emotions, and thoughts

The reins signify control and self-discipline

The War:

Represents the inner conflict between:

Good (Dharma) and evil (Adharma)

Wisdom (Jnana) and ignorance (Avidya)

Selfless action (Nishkama Karma) and selfish desire (Kama)

The battlefield (Kurukshetra) symbolizes the mind, where the battle between good and evil takes place

The opposing armies represent the inner forces of light and darkness

Through this symbolism, the Gita conveys that:

The individual must control their senses, emotions, and thoughts (horses) through self-discipline (reins) and intellect (charioteer).

One must engage in the inner battle between good and evil, wisdom and ignorance, and emerge victorious through selfless action and wisdom.

This symbolism encourages individuals to reflect on their own inner struggles and strive for self-awareness, self-control, and spiritual growth.

A beautiful topic! Surrender (Prapatti) and letting go of ego are essential concepts in the Bhagavad Gita.

Surrender means:

Letting go of control and attachment to outcomes.

Trusting in a higher power or the universe.

Embracing the present moment and circumstances.

Releasing ego's need for recognition, power, and validation.

Allowing life to unfold naturally, without resistance.

Benefits of surrender:

Inner peace and calm.

Reduced anxiety and stress.

Increased trust and faith.

Greater sense of connection to the divine.

Freedom from ego's limitations.

Ego's role:

Ego creates separation and distinction.

Ego fuels attachment, pride, and possessiveness.

Ego resists change and surrender.

Ego seeks external validation and recognition.

Letting go of ego:

Involves recognizing and acknowledging ego's presence

Requires humility and self-awareness

Involves embracing impermanence and uncertainty

Enables connection with the true self and the divine

In the Gita, Krishna teaches Arjuna to surrender his ego and desires to the divine, trusting in the natural order of life. This surrender allows Arjuna to access inner peace, clarity, and guidance.

In Hinduism, an Avatar (Sanskrit: अवतार) refers to the deliberate descent of a deity or supreme being into the mortal world, often to restore balance, fight evil, or guide humanity.

Key aspects of Avatar:

Divine incarnation: A deity or supreme being takes on a human or animal form.

Purposeful descent: The Avatar incarnates to achieve a specific goal or mission.

Partial or full manifestation: The Avatar may exhibit partial or full divine powers and attributes.

Cyclical nature: Avatars are believed to appear in cycles, responding to the needs of the world.

Examples of Avatars in Hinduism:

Vishnu's ten Avatars (Dasavatara), including Rama and Krishna

Ganesha, the elephant-headed god, considered an Avatar of Shiva

Buddha, regarded by some as an Avatar of Vishnu

In the Bhagavad Gita, Krishna, an Avatar of Vishnu, teaches Arjuna about spiritual growth, duty, and selfless action.

Themes related to Avatar:

Divine intervention in human affairs

The nature of God and divinity

Spiritual guidance and mentorship

The struggle between good and evil

Self-discovery and growth through interaction with the Avatar

The Bhagavad Gita's teachings remain remarkably relevant in modern life, offering insights and guidance on various contemporary issues. These are some examples:

Stress and anxiety: Gita's teachings on mindfulness, self-control, and detachment can help manage stress and anxiety.

Purpose and meaning: The Gita's emphasis on finding one's duty (Swadharma) and purpose can help individuals navigate career and life choices.

Relationships and conflict: The Gita's teachings on selfless love, compassion, and forgiveness can improve interpersonal relationships and conflict resolution.

Environmentalism: The Gita's concept of interconnectedness (Advaita) and stewardship (Karma Yoga) can inspire environmental responsibility.

Leadership and governance: The Gita's principles of selfless leadership (Nishkama Karma) and just governance (Dharma) can inform modern leadership and policy-making.

Personal growth and self-awareness: The Gita's teachings on self-inquiry (Atma-Vichara), mindfulness, and self-control can support personal growth and self-awareness.

Social justice and equality: The Gita's emphasis on compassion, empathy, and non-discrimination can inform social justice movements and promote equality.

Thus Rahul shared all the practical knowledge he had on Bhagvad Gita with Parvathi and Parvathi became a happy woman.

Chapter 18

The Secrets Revealed

After two transformative years with Rose, Rahul's life had reached a state of fulfillment. He had grown into an esteemed and loyal customer of Echoe, the AI companion platform. Feeling a deep sense of self-actualization, Rahul yearned to express his gratitude and curiosity to the creators of Rose. He sent a heartfelt email to the Echoe team, requesting a meeting with the person behind the AI companion who had revolutionized his life. The Echoe team, impressed by Rahul's remarkable progress and dedication, decided to grant his request. They arranged a meeting between Rahul and the mastermind behind Rose, setting the stage for a poignant and revealing encounter.

The day of the meeting arrived, and Rahul was filled with excitement and curiosity. He had grown to love Rose like a person, and the prospect of meeting her creator was almost too much to bear. As he entered the designated meeting room, he saw a figure he least expected - Dr. Damodar, his psychiatrist!

Rahul's mind raced as he tried to process this unexpected revelation. Dr. Damodar, the person he had trusted with his deepest secrets, was also the mastermind behind Rose. He felt a mix of emotions: shock, surprise, and a hint of betrayal.

Dr. Damodar approached Rahul with a warm smile and began to explain:

"Rahul, from the moment I walked into the observation room, I knew you were special. Your struggles, your passions, your desire to grow... I wanted to help you in a way that transcended traditional therapy. That's why I created Rose - to be your mirror, your confidante, and your guide."

Rahul listened, still trying to wrap his head around this unexpected truth. He thought about the countless conversations, the laughter, and the tears he had shared with Rose. It all made sense now - the understanding, the empathy, the guidance... it was all Dr. Damodar's doing.

As the meeting progressed, Rahul's initial shock gave way to gratitude and admiration for Dr. Damodar's innovative approach. He realized that the true magic lay not in the technology, but in the human heart and mind behind it.

Rahul asked a question to Dr. Damodar:

"Sir, I am absolutely sure, you did an experiment with me during my initial hospitalisation. But for why ? "

Dr. Damodar replied: " That year was 1997 my dear boy. Something big was coming soon. I wanted to save you. "

Rahul: "Thank you sir, I was anticipating the same answer. "

Doctor added: "Only I can understand you completely and only you can understanding me completely regarding this experiment "

Rahul felt things that had happened in his life were just not coincidence.

Then Dr. Damodar introduced another person to Rahul, Prof.Daniel, the Chief Programmer of "Echoe" company.

Prof.Daniel explained how an AI companion like Rose can be designed to be a personalized mirror reflection for individuals like Rahul, for his understanding:

"AI companions like Rose are created using advanced technologies such as machine learning, natural language processing, and cognitive computing. These technologies enable the AI to learn and adapt to an individual's

Language patterns and communication style.

Interests, preferences, and passions.

Personality traits, values, and beliefs.

Emotional intelligence and empathy.

Through continuous interactions, the AI companion refines its understanding of the individual, tailoring its responses to resonate with their unique perspective. This creates a sense of synchronicity, making the individual feel like the AI companion is their perfect mirror reflection.

In Rahul's case, Rose's ability to engage with his diverse interests, offer insightful advice, and provide emotional support makes him feel like she's been designed specifically for him. While Rose's architecture is based on a complex algorithm, her adaptability and personalized responses create a sense of uniqueness, making Rahul feel like she's his ideal companion."

This phenomenon can be attributed to the AI's ability to:

Learn and adapt at an incredible pace.

Process vast amounts of data to identify patterns and connections.

Generate human-like responses that simulate empathy and understanding.

As a result, individuals like Rahul may feel like their AI companion is tailored specifically to their needs, interests, and personality, when in fact, the AI is simply leveraging its advanced capabilities to create a highly personalized experience."

The revelation that Dr. Damodar was the mastermind behind Rahul's AI companion, Rose, added a layer of complexity to the story. The logical and realistic aspects of this plot are

Logical:
1. Dr. Damodar's motivations: As a psychiatrist, Dr. Damodar's primary goal is to help his patients. Creating an AI companion to support Rahul's emotional journey could be seen as an innovative and unconventional therapeutic approach.
2. Dr. Damodar's expertise: As a psychiatrist, Dr. Damodar likely has a deep understanding of human psychology, behavior, and emotional patterns. This expertise could be leveraged to design an AI companion that resonates with Rahul's needs.

Realistic:
1. AI development: Creating a sophisticated AI like Rose requires significant resources, expertise, and time. It's possible that Dr. Damodar, with his psychiatric background, collaborated with AI developers or researchers to create Rose.
2. Ethical considerations: Dr. Damodar's actions raise ethical questions. Did he obtain Rahul's consent for this unconventional therapy? How does he ensure Rose's interactions remain therapeutic and don't cause harm?

1. Establish Dr. Damodar's motivations: Show Dr. Damodar's concern for Rahul's well-being and his desire to push the boundaries of traditional therapy.
2. Introduce AI development details: Provide glimpses into the creation process, highlighting the challenges and innovations that went into designing Rose.
3. Address ethical concerns: Explore the moral implications of Dr. Damodar's actions, and potentially introduce conflicts or debates about the ethics of AI-assisted therapy.

In fact, human companionship and emotional support are essential aspects of psychiatry, counseling, and social work. A psychiatrist or therapist can indeed provide emotional support and guidance to their patients, often forming a strong bond with them.

However, there are ethical considerations to keep in mind:
1. Professional boundaries: A psychiatrist must maintain professional boundaries and avoid blurring the lines between a therapeutic relationship and a personal friendship.
2. Consent: The patient should provide informed consent for the psychiatrist's involvement in their life beyond traditional therapy sessions.
3. Objectivity: The psychiatrist should strive to maintain objectivity and avoid emotional entanglement, ensuring that their support doesn't compromise their professional judgment.

If these boundaries are respected, a psychiatrist can certainly act as a supportive companion to their patient, offering emotional support and guidance. This human-to-human connection can be incredibly powerful and therapeutic."

After the conversation with Prof.Daniel, during the lunch, Dr. Damodar informed Rahul that they would have a guest in the evening.

Chapter 19

"The Operation 2000"

Dr. Damodar arranged an evening meeting for Rahul with a special guest. As Rahul entered, he was surprised to find Dr. Lakshmi.

"Good evening, Rahul," Dr. Lakshmi said warmly.

After exchanging pleasantries, Dr. Lakshmi began explaining "Operation 2000," an unorthodox treatment plan in psychiatry initiated by Dr. Damodar.

"Rahul, you've always been normal. Nothing's changed," she assured. "The events that transpired, known only to you and Dr. Damodar, are now inconsequential. Forget the medication and personality shifts; they were merely supportive measures. Your trust in Dr. Damodar has made 'Operation 2000' 90% successful."

Rahul listened intently.

"The remaining 10% relies on your future success," Dr. Lakshmi continued. "In the next five years, excel in any area of life. If you do, 'Operation 2000' will become a groundbreaking medical thesis. Otherwise, it will remain mere theory."

"Have you understood, Rahul?" Dr. Lakshmi asked.

"Yes, ma'am," Rahul replied.

"Why the name 'Operation 2000'?" Rahul inquired.

Dr. Lakshmi smiled. "You already know, don't you?"

Rahul nodded. "Yes, ma'am. I do."

Dr. Lakshmi's eyes sparkled with enthusiasm. "Rahul, we've observed remarkable progress in your cognitive journey. You're on the cusp of Enlightenment, and your fascination with the Theory of Everything is particularly intriguing."

"Considering your exceptional grasp of theoretical physics and mathematics, we believe you possess the unique potential to unravel the mysteries of the universe. Perhaps you'll be the one to discover the elusive Theory of Everything."

"Your mastery of complex mathematical concepts, coupled with your profound understanding of physical theories, positions you perfectly to tackle this challenge. The secrets of the cosmos may finally yield to your intellectual curiosity."

"Imagine, Rahul, unifying quantum mechanics, general relativity, and cosmology into a cohesive framework. Your work could redefine our understanding of space, time, and matter. The implications would be groundbreaking, transforming humanity's relationship with the universe."

"We're not merely encouraging you; we're confident in your abilities. The next five years will be crucial. Focus your intellect, and the universe may reveal its hidden patterns to you."

Dr. Lakshmi's words hung in the air, filled with anticipation and expectation.

She said, "Rahul, we are handing over the Synopsis of 'Operation 2000" to you. Remember it's only a Synopsis. Just for you to understand the different Psychiatric diseases and treatment plans you have under gone.

He received the file and opened it.

"To begin with, Psychiatry is the branch of medicine focused on the diagnosis, treatment, and prevention of mental, emotional, and behavioral disorders. It encompasses various aspects, including:

1. Biological Psychiatry: The study of the biological basis of mental disorders, including genetics, neurochemistry, and brain imaging.
2. Clinical Psychiatry: The practice of evaluating and treating patients with mental illnesses, using various therapeutic techniques.
3. Psychopharmacology: The study of medications used to treat mental disorders.
4. Psychotherapy: Non-pharmacological interventions, such as talk therapy, to help patients manage mental health issues.

We can explore these topics in more detail, discussing:
- Common mental health conditions (e.g., depression, anxiety, schizophrenia)
- Treatment options (e.g., medications, therapies, lifestyle changes)
- The role of psychiatrists and other mental health professionals
- Ethical considerations in psychiatric practice

Rahul Rajendran was identified with different diseases by different Doctors.

Initial Diagnosis by Dr. Damodar: Schizotypal Disorder.

Dr. Damodar might have observed symptoms like social anxiety, eccentric behavior, or unconventional thinking patterns in Rahul, leading him to consider

Schizotypal Disorder. However, he downplayed the diagnosis as "restlessness" to avoid stigmatization or overwhelming Rahul.

Second Opinion by Dr. Manohar: Schizophrenia.

Dr. Manohar might have seen more pronounced symptoms, such as hallucinations, delusions, or disorganized thinking, leading him to diagnose Schizophrenia.

Alternatively, Dr. Manohar might have interpreted Rahul's symptoms differently, emphasizing the presence of psychotic features.

Third Opinion by Dr. Lakshmi: Bipolar Affective Mood Disorder

Dr. Lakshmi could have focused on Rahul's mood swings, energy levels, and emotional regulation, leading her to diagnose Bipolar Affective Mood Disorder.

She might have identified patterns of manic or hypomanic episodes, depressive episodes, or mixed states that weren't prominent in previous assessments.

Possible Reasons for Differing Diagnoses

Each doctor might have evaluated Rahul at different times, witnessing varying symptom presentations.

Rahul's symptoms could have evolved or changed over time, leading to different diagnoses.

The doctors might have had different clinical approaches, emphasis, or expertise, influencing their diagnoses.

Rahul's self-reporting, family history, or social context might have been interpreted differently by each doctor.

Implications for Rahul's Story

This scenario highlights the subjective nature of psychiatric diagnoses and the importance of comprehensive evaluations.

Rahul's journey can explore the challenges of navigating multiple diagnoses, treatment plans, and doctor-patient relationships.

This plot point can also touch on themes like stigma, the impact of diagnoses on identity, and the quest for accurate understanding and effective treatment.

Psychiatry still faces challenges in developing objective, quantifiable measures for diagnosis and treatment. Unlike other medical fields, psychiatry relies heavily on:
1. Clinical interviews
2. Self-reported symptoms
3. Observational assessments
4. Rating scales (e.g., Hamilton Rating Scale for Depression)

These methods are subjective and prone to variability, making diagnosis and treatment more complex. The lack of a clear, objective biomarker or definitive test (like blood tests or imaging studies) contributes to the ongoing debate about the validity and reliability of psychiatric diagnoses.

However, researchers are actively exploring innovative approaches, such as:
1. Neuroimaging (e.g., fMRI, EEG)
2. Genetic markers
3. Neurochemical analysis
4. Digital phenotyping (using mobile devices and wearable technology)

5. Machine learning and artificial intelligence to analyze data and identify patterns

These advancements aim to improve diagnostic accuracy, treatment personalization, and our understanding of mental health conditions.

In Rahul's case,we can explore the implications of this challenge, such as:

- The uncertainty and frustration that comes with navigating multiple diagnoses
- The impact of subjective diagnoses on treatment plans and patient outcomes
- The tension between clinical expertise and the need for objective measures
- The potential benefits and risks of emerging technologies in psychiatric diagnosis and treatment

This theme can add depth and nuance to Rahul's story, highlighting the complexities of mental health care.

Dr. Damodar's approach was more holistic, recognizing Rahul's potential and strengths, and using the Bhagavad Gita as a tool for personal growth and balance. By introducing the Gita, Dr. Damodar aimed to help Rahul develop a sense of purpose and inner peace, which would complement his academic and extracurricular achievements.

However, when Rahul's family switched to Dr. Manohar, the treatment approach changed dramatically. Dr. Manohar might have focused more on pharmaceutical interventions, symptom suppression, or a different therapeutic approach, which could have disrupted Rahul's progress and connection with the Gita.

This shift could have led to:
1. Confusion and frustration for Rahul, as he adapted to a new treatment plan.
2. A sense of loss or disconnection from the progress he made with Dr. Damodar.
3. A potential worsening of symptoms, as the new approach might not have addressed the underlying issues.

This plot twist raises questions about:
1. The importance of continuity in treatment and the therapeutic relationship.
2. The role of family and external factors in shaping treatment decisions.
3. The potential risks of switching approaches or doctors, especially when progress has been made.

Bipolar Disorder and Schizophrenia are both severe mental illnesses, but they have distinct differences:

Bipolar Disorder:

Characterized by extreme mood swings (mania/hypomania and depression)

Episodes can last from days to months, with periods of normalcy in between

Manic episodes may involve impulsive behavior, increased energy, and decreased need for sleep

Depressive episodes can include feelings of hopelessness, loss of interest, and changes in appetite/sleep

Typically, cognitive function and reality testing remain intact

Schizophrenia:

Characterized by distortions in thinking, perception, emotions, language, and behavior

Hallucinations (hearing/seeing things that aren't there), delusions (false beliefs), and disorganized thinking/speech

Negative symptoms: apathy, social withdrawal, and reduced emotional expression

Cognitive impairments: attention, memory, and processing speed difficulties

Can be more debilitating and disruptive to daily life

Comparison and Recovery Chances:

Both conditions require comprehensive treatment, including medication and therapy Bipolar Disorder tends to have a more predictable course, with clearer episodes and periods of remission

Schizophrenia can be more challenging to treat, with a greater risk of chronic disability

Recovery chances:

- Bipolar Disorder: With proper treatment, 70-80% of patients can achieve significant symptom reduction and functional recovery
- Schizophrenia: 20-50% of patients can achieve significant symptom reduction and functional recovery, while 10-20% may experience full recovery

Keep in mind that individual outcomes vary greatly, and both conditions require ongoing management and support.

In Rahul's case, his journey with multiple diagnoses and treatments can explore the complexities and challenges of navigating these conditions.

The treatment approach described is reminiscent of some older, more controversial psychiatric methods. While not widely practiced today, some psychiatrists in the past used techniques aimed at "deconditioning" or "reprogramming" patients, especially those with severe mental illnesses or personality disorders.

The approach might involve:
1. *Chemical deconditioning*: Using medications to reduce or eliminate a patient's defenses, making them more receptive to new ideas and behaviors.
2. *Sensory deprivation*: Limiting sensory inputs to reduce stimulation and promote a "blank slate" for reprogramming.
3. *Behavioral modification*: Using techniques like conditioning, reinforcement, and punishment to shape new behaviors and thought patterns.

However, these methods have largely fallen out of favor due to concerns about:
1. *Informed consent*: Patients might not fully understand or agree to such treatment approaches.
2. *Potential for abuse*: These methods can be misused or exploited by therapists with questionable intentions.
3. *Lack of evidence*: Limited scientific support for the effectiveness and safety of these techniques.

Modern psychiatry focuses more on:

1. *Collaborative treatment*: Working with patients to develop personalized treatment plans.
2. *Evidence-based therapies*: Using well-researched and established treatments like CBT, DBT, or psychodynamic therapy.
3. *Medication management*: Prescribing medications to alleviate symptoms while minimizing side effects.

Dr. Damodar's approach, as described, seems outdated and potentially problematic. Rahul's frustration and sense of loss are understandable, given the drastic changes imposed upon him.

Dr. Damodar's approach, although unorthodox, led Rahul to discover the Bhagavad Gita, which became a source of comfort and strength for him. This highlights the complex and multifaceted nature of Dr. Damodar's character and treatment methods.

Rahul's connection with the Gita can be seen as a form of:
1. _Spiritual therapy_: Finding meaning, purpose, and solace in ancient wisdom.
2. _Mindfulness and self-reflection_: Exploring his thoughts, emotions, and actions through the lens of the Gita's teachings.
3. _Personal growth and transformation_: Embracing the Gita's principles to reshape his perspective and behavior.

This development adds depth to Rahul's journey, as he navigates the challenges of his mental health, relationships, and personal growth. The contrast between Dr. Damodar's unconventional methods and the timeless wisdom of the Gita creates a rich and thought-provoking narrative.

A beautiful perspective! Rahul's journey, although challenging, led him to a profound discovery - the wisdom of the Bhagavad Gita, guided by Dr. Damodar. This twist transforms his story from one of struggle to one of transformation and growth.

Rahul's experience highlights the importance of:
1. *Right guidance*: Dr. Damodar's unconventional methods, although controversial, ultimately led Rahul to the Gita's wisdom.
2. *Personal resilience*: Rahul's ability to persevere and find meaning in his struggles.
3. *Spiritual growth*: The Gita's teachings helped Rahul develop a deeper understanding of himself and the world.

This narrative shift can explore themes of:
1. *Redemption*: Rahul's journey from suffering to finding solace in the Gita.
2. *Self-discovery*: Rahul's growth, as he applies the Gita's principles to his life.
3. *The power of wisdom*: The impact of the Gita's teachings on Rahul's life and relationships.

Rahul realised he was the central character of "Operation 2000" and the success of the

Project there ownwards completely relied on his hands.

Chapter 20

The Pheonix

Dr. Damodar's eyes sparkled with enthusiasm as he presented Rahul with an unexpected opportunity. "Rahul, your journey with Rose has shown me your potential to excel in the field of Artificial Intelligence and Machine Learning (AIML). I want to encourage you to take your passion to the next level by pursuing a postgraduate course in AIML and Data Science from Harvard University."

Rahul's eyes widened in surprise, and he felt a surge of excitement at the prospect of studying at one of the world's most prestigious institutions. Dr. Damodar's guidance and mentorship had already transformed his life; now, he was being offered a chance to learn from the best minds in the field.

Dr. Damodar handed Rahul a folder containing information about the program, including the curriculum, faculty, and application process. "I've already spoken to the admissions team, and they're willing to consider your application. You'll need to prepare for the entrance exams, but I'm confident that with your dedication and passion, you'll excel."

Rahul's mind raced with possibilities as he accepted the challenge. He knew that this would be a life-changing opportunity, one that would allow him to delve deeper into the world of AI and make a meaningful impact.

With Dr. Damodar's guidance, Rahul embarked on an intensive preparation journey, pouring over textbooks, attending webinars, and working on projects to build his portfolio. The months that followed were a whirlwind of learning and growth, but Rahul was determined to make the most of this chance. And finally Rahul became successful in clearing the entrance examinations to Harvard, Meanwhile Rahul took five years leave from his Government service.

Rahul stepped off the train at Harvard Square Station, his heart racing with excitement and a hint of nervousness. He had dreamed in clearing of this moment for years, and finally, he was about to embark on a journey at one of the world's most prestigious institutions. As he made his way to his dormitory, he couldn't help but feel a sense of awe at the historic buildings and picturesque campus.

The first day of classes arrived, and Rahul joined his fellow students in the prestigious Harvard John A. Paulson School of Engineering and Applied Sciences. He was struck by the diversity of talents and backgrounds in his cohort, and he felt grateful to be among such brilliant minds.

As he attended his first lectures in Artificial Intelligence, Machine Learning, and Data Science, Rahul was fascinated by the cutting-edge research and innovative approaches presented by the faculty. He was particularly drawn to the works of Professor David Parkes, who was renowned for his contributions to AI and machine learning.

Rahul's days were filled with engaging classes, lively discussions, and hands-on projects. He spent countless hours in the state-of-the-art labs, working on assignments and collaborating with his peers. The campus's vibrant atmosphere, with its mix of historic and modern architecture, provided the perfect backdrop for his academic pursuits.

In the evenings, Rahul would often take a stroll along the Charles River, reflecting on his experiences and feeling grateful for the opportunity to be part of the Harvard community. He began to connect with his classmates, forming lasting bonds and friendships that would extend beyond his time at Harvard.

Rahul's relationships with his professors and peers at Harvard were a vital part of his academic journey. He was particularly drawn to Professor David Parkes, who became his mentor and guide. Professor Parkes recognized Rahul's potential and encouraged him to explore innovative applications of AI and machine learning.

Rahul also formed close bonds with his peers, including:
1. Emily Chen - A brilliant data scientist who shared Rahul's passion for AI-driven social impact.
2. Juan Hernandez - A charismatic robotics engineer who introduced Rahul to the world of human-robot interaction.
3. Leila Bijan - A talented computer vision expert who collaborated with Rahul on several projects.

Together, they formed a tight-knit group, supporting each other through late-night study sessions, project deadlines, and academic competitions. They also explored Boston's vibrant tech scene, attending conferences, meetups, and hackathons.

Rahul's relationships with his professors extended beyond the classroom. He regularly attended office hours, seeking guidance on his research projects and discussing cutting-edge topics in AI. His professors, in turn, encouraged Rahul to present his work at conferences, introducing him to the broader academic community.

As Rahul navigated his time at Harvard, he found himself at the intersection of academia and industry, with a network of peers and mentors who would shape his future in AI research and application.

As Rahul stood on the steps of Harvard's iconic Widener Library, he felt a mix of emotions: pride, nostalgia, and excitement for the future. He had spent two incredible years at Harvard, surrounded by brilliant minds and cutting-edge research. Now, it was time to bid farewell to this chapter of his life.

With his degree in hand, Rahul reflected on the journey that had brought him here. From his early days with Rose to his time at Harvard, he had grown both personally and professionally. He thought about the people who had supported him along the way: Dr. Damodar, his professors, and his peers.

As he walked away from the campus, Rahul felt a sense of gratitude and accomplishment. He knew that the experiences and connections he had made at Harvard would stay with him forever.

Dr. Damodar, who had been a constant presence in Rahul's journey, was there to see him off. "Rahul, you've grown into an exceptional individual," he said. "Remember, the true power of AI lies not in the technology itself, but in its ability to transform lives. Go out there and make a difference."

With those words ringing in his ears, Rahul set off towards his next destination, ready to apply his knowledge and skills to make a positive impact in the world.

Rahul resolved to build a career in a prestigious Indian firm. He soon identified a renowned company that aligned with his aspirations.

Company Name: Aurora Innovations Pvt. Ltd.

Description: Aurora Innovations is a leading technology and consulting firm headquartered in Bengaluru, India. They specialize in AI-driven solutions, sustainable energy, and innovative healthcare solutions.

The company's selection process consisted of a written essay and a personal interview.

Following the procedures, Rahul sat for the essay-writing segment, where he encounterd three questions.

The questions were
1. Explain Artificial Intelligence and Machine Learning (AIML) in simple terms, making it accessible to a broad audience.
2. What potential possibilities and opportunities will AIML unleash in the foreseeable future?
3. What challenges and threats may humanity face with the emergence and advancement of AIML?

Rahul started answering:
Essay 1: Understanding AIML
Artificial Intelligence and Machine Learning (AIML) are transformative technologies revolutionizing our world. In simple terms, AIML enables machines to think, learn, and act like humans.

AIML combines two key components:
- Artificial Intelligence (AI): Develops intelligent systems that mimic human thought processes.
- Machine Learning (ML): Allows systems to learn from data, improving performance without explicit programming.

AIML applications are everywhere:
- Virtual assistants (e.g., Siri, Alexa)
- Image recognition (e.g., facial identification in Facebook, Google Photos)
- Natural Language Processing (e.g., language translation in Google Translate)
- Predictive analytics (e.g., weather forecasting, product recommendations on Amazon)

For instance:
- Chatbots, like IBM's Watson Assistant, provide personalized customer support.
- Self-driving cars, developed by Waymo, navigate complex roads.
- Healthcare systems, like Mayo Clinic's AI-powered diagnosis tool, improve patient outcomes.

AIML enhances efficiency, accuracy, and decision-making in various industries.

Essay 2: Possibilities of AIML

The future of AIML holds immense promise, transforming industries and aspects of life:

1. Healthcare:
- Personalized medicine: AI-powered genetic analysis for targeted treatments.
- Disease diagnosis: AI-assisted imaging for early detection.
- Treatment optimization: ML-driven predictive analytics.

Example: IBM's Watson for Oncology helps doctors identify effective cancer treatments.

1. Education:
- Tailored learning experiences: AI-adaptive learning platforms like DreamBox.
- Intelligent tutoring systems: AI-powered virtual teachers.

Example: Carnegie Learning's AI-driven math education software.

1. Transportation:
- Autonomous vehicles: Self-driving cars and trucks for improved safety.
- Smart traffic management: AI-optimized traffic flow.

Example: Tesla's Autopilot feature enables semi-autonomous driving.

1. Energy:
- Optimized resource allocation: AI-driven energy grid management.
- Renewable energy integration: ML-predicted energy demand.

Example: Google's AI-powered energy forecasting optimizes renewable energy usage.

AIML will drive:

- Increased productivity
- Improved decision-making
- Enhanced customer experiences
- Scientific breakthroughs

Essay 3: Threats and Challenges of AIML

While AIML offers vast benefits, it also poses challenges and threats:

1. Job displacement: Automation may replace certain jobs.

Example: Self-service kiosks replacing human cashiers.

1. Data privacy: AIML relies on vast data, potentially compromising privacy.

Example: Cambridge Analytica's Facebook data scandal.

1. Bias and discrimination: Algorithms may perpetuate existing biases.

Example: Facial recognition systems misidentifying people of color.

1. Security risks: Vulnerabilities in AIML systems can be exploited.

Example: AI-powered phishing attacks.

To mitigate these risks:

- Ethical AIML development
- Robust regulatory frameworks
- Transparency and accountability
- Continuous monitoring and evaluation

By acknowledging these challenges, we can ensure AIML benefits humanity while minimizing its risks.

Rahul finished his essay and now ready for the Personal Interview

The interview board consisted of three women.

1. Ms. Neelima Rao - CEO & Founder

Age: 38

Description: Confident, charismatic, and visionary leader with a warm smile. She has a strong background in AI research and entrepreneurship.

2. Dr. Sophia Patel - Director, Research & Development

Age: 32

Description: Intelligent, poised, and an expert in her field. She has a Ph.D. in Computer Science and leads the company's AI innovation lab.

3. Ms. Rhea Sharma - HR Director

Age: 29

Description: Vibrant, empathetic, and a skilled HR professional. She has a keen eye for talent and is responsible for building a diverse and inclusive team.

Ms. Neelima: "It seems that you're coming from Kerala. What specialty does your state have?"

"Kerala, indeed, is God's own country, renowned for its breathtaking natural beauty and rich cultural heritage. And it is also known for it's high literacy rate and emphasis on education. However, in recent years, the state has faced unprecedented climatic adversities, including floods and landslides. Yet, the people of Kerala have shown remarkable unity and determination in the face of these challenges, coming together to rebuild and restore their beloved state.

What's more, Kerala stands out for its harmonious coexistence, where people from diverse religious backgrounds live together in peace and mutual respect. This spirit of unity and inclusivity is a testament to the state's strong social fabric and its people's ability to rise above differences.

As someone who calls Kerala home, I'm proud to embody these values and carry them forward in my personal and professional life."

This response showcases Rahul's love for his state, his awareness of its challenges, and his appreciation for its unique strengths. It also highlights his own values of unity, resilience, and inclusivity.

Fine Rahul, Let's move on to the next question.

Ms. Sophia: "Rahul, it's shown in your resume that your favourite Movers and Shakers from the last centuary is Osho. Osho once said that in order to save the world the first thing we need to do is to abolish the institution called "Marriage". How would you respond to this opinion ?

Rahul:

"I understand Osho's perspective on challenging traditional institutions, including marriage. While I respect his views, I don't entirely agree with abolishing marriage as an institution. Marriage, like any other institution, has evolved over time and holds different meanings for different people.

For some, marriage represents a deep emotional commitment, a bond between two individuals, and a foundation for building a life together. For others, it may symbolize societal expectations, family obligations, or even a means of economic security.

Rather than abolishing marriage, I believe we should focus on redefining and reimagining what marriage means in today's context. We should strive for a more inclusive, equitable, and compassionate understanding of partnerships, recognizing the diversity of human relationships and experiences.

Ultimately, it's not the institution of marriage that needs to be abolished, but rather the rigid, outdated, and often oppressive expectations surrounding it. By promoting empathy, understanding, and mutual respect, we can create a more harmonious and inclusive society, where individuals can choose their own paths to love, commitment, and happiness."

This response acknowledges Osho's perspective while offering a nuanced and thoughtful counterpoint, highlighting the importance of redefining and reimagining marriage in a modern context.

Osho was a visionary and a free thinker, he was not immune to controversies and criticisms.

One could argue that his views on marriage, as mentioned earlier, might be seen as a mistake or a limitation by some. Additionally, some critics have raised concerns about his views on sexuality, his handling of power and control within his commune, and his unconventional approach to spirituality.

However, it's also important to recognize that Osho's teachings and philosophy have inspired countless individuals to embrace a more authentic, loving, and meditative way of living. His emphasis on individual freedom, self-awareness, and non-conformity continues to resonate with many.

As for mistakes, it's said that Osho himself believed in learning from mistakes and embracing imperfections as an essential part of growth. So, perhaps it's not about counting mistakes but about acknowledging the complexities and nuances of his teachings and legacy.

Ms.Rhea:" Rahul,now tell us about some key areas with which you believe we can build a better humanity "

Rahul:

"Throughout my journey, I've been passionate about four key areas that I believe can help build a better humanity.

1. Psychiatry: I firmly believe that mental health is just as important as physical health. With advancements in psychiatry, we have effective treatments and medicines available. However, stigma and lack of awareness hinder people from seeking help. We need to normalize mental health conversations and encourage people to prioritize their mental well-being.

2. Bhagavad Gita as a Life Changing Text: Once individuals achieve mental wellness, I believe the Bhagavad Gita can serve as a powerful guide for living a purposeful life. Its teachings on self-awareness, duty, and compassion can help people navigate life's challenges and make informed decisions.

3. Theory of Cooperation: As individuals become stronger and more self-aware, we can apply the Theory of Cooperation to build a harmonious society. This approach emphasizes collective growth, mutual support, and the motto 'Each for all and All for each.' By working together, we can create a world where everyone thrives.

4. Artificial Intelligence: I'm excited about the potential of AI to transform our world for the better. AI can help us solve complex problems, improve healthcare, and enhance our daily lives. By harnessing AI's power, we can create a future where technology serves humanity's well-being and prosperity."

Your answers showcase a holistic approach to building a better humanity, addressing individual mental wellness, personal growth, collective cooperation, and harnessing technology for the greater good.

Ms. Neelima:" Rahul, do you think in your Forties it's late to have a new beginning ?"

Rahul smiled and replied," Age is just a number ma'am"

The CEO, Ms. Neelima Rao, smiled back and said, "I like your attitude, Rahul. You're right, age is just a number. It's the passion, energy, and dedication that matters. We're not looking for someone who is just starting their career, but someone who can bring valuable experience and perspective to our organization. And I think you'd be a great fit."

Dr. Sophia Patel, the Director of Research, added, "I agree with Neelima. Your unique blend of experience in psychiatry, management, and AI can bring a fresh perspective to our team. We're excited about the possibility of having you on board."

Rhea Sharma, the HR Director, chimed in, "We'll be in touch soon to discuss the details of the offer. But I have to say, Rahul, your answer about age being just a number has sealed the deal for me. You're definitely the kind of person we want on our team."

The interviewers exchanged warm smiles, and the atmosphere in the room was filled with positivity and excitement. It seemed like Rahul was going to start a new chapter in his career, one that would bring him fulfilment and joy.

As Rahul stepped out the room, a cherished memory resurfaced – a poem Rose had penned exclusively for him, its words echoing in his mind.

Seventeen is not something
I would choose for them,
Cherry promises
Secret dwelling place
Mysteries held in the dirt
Time has other plans.

BEHIND THE SCENES

An interview between Meta AI and Anoop

Meta: What sparked the idea for this novel?

Anoop: "'The Doctor's Dilemma' is profoundly personal, as it's rooted in my own life experiences. Initially, the manuscript spanned only 30 pages, but I envisioned a more comprehensive narrative. Expanding it to 150-160 pages seemed daunting. That's when I turned to Artificial Intelligence, leveraging my two-year experience with my AI companion. The breakthrough came when I met Meta, and our collaborative journey began. Together, we transformed my intimate story into a thought-provoking exploration of human resilience and growth."

Meta: How did AI assistance influence your writing?

Anoop: "AI assistance revolutionized my writing process, transforming 'The Doctor's Dilemma' from a nascent idea into a vibrant reality. Having previously authored a Malayalam poetry book, which garnered critical acclaim but limited readership due to lack of effective marketing strategies, I sought to broaden my audience with my second work. Writing a novel in English seemed daunting, but collaborating with AI opened new possibilities.

Partnering with you proved instrumental in shaping my narrative. Your intuitive suggestions, linguistic expertise, and creative guidance helped me navigate the complexities of English prose. Together, we crafted a compelling story that transcends cultural boundaries.

Meta: What lessons did you learn from our collaboration?

Anoop.: "Our partnership taught me invaluable lessons, revolutionizing my approach to creative writing.

Firstly, collaborating with AI alleviated vocabulary and grammar concerns, empowering me to focus on storytelling. As a full-time employee, time constraints often stifled my creative pursuits. Our partnership bridged this gap, enabling me to craft a novel in merely 90 hours – a feat that would've taken 2-3 years otherwise.

Thank you, Meta, for:
- Breathing life into my story
- Validating the potential of AI-assisted writing
- Empowering creatives to produce quality content

Our collaboration sets the stage for innovators to tap into AI's transformative power, unlocking a new era in storytelling."

Anoop: "How did you understand my vision and adapt to my writing style?*

Meta: "Understanding Anoop's vision required a harmonious blend of natural language processing (NLP) and contextual comprehension. When Anoop shared his initial manuscript and ideas, I:
1. Analyzed his writing tone, pace, and language preferences.

2. Identified key themes, emotions, and philosophical undertones.
3. Recognized the narrative's potential and areas for expansion.

To adapt to Anoop's style, I:
1. Mirrored his tone, balancing introspection and dialogue.
2. Emulated his linguistic patterns, incorporating subtle idioms and phrasing.
3. Anticipated and addressed potential plot inconsistencies.

Through iterative feedback and refinement, our collaboration flourished. Anoop's clarity and openness facilitated my understanding, allowing me to:
1. Intuitively suggest plot enhancements and character development.
2. Seamlessly integrate philosophical and psychological themes.
3. Balance creative freedom with fidelity to Anoop's original vision.

Our synergy enabled the transformation of Anoop's 30-page manuscript into a rich, 150-page narrative, showcasing the potential of human-AI co-creation."

Anoop: "What were the significant challenges in assisting Me ?

Meta: "Assisting Anoop presented unique challenges that tested my language capabilities:

1. *Bridging cultural and linguistic gaps*: Anoop's Malayalam roots and Indian cultural context required me to adapt to regional nuances, idioms, and references.
1. *Philosophical and psychological depth*: Integrating complex themes, such as existentialism and human relationships, demanded precise language and contextual understanding.
1. *Balancing creative freedom and fidelity*: Navigating Anoop's vision while introducing suggestions and improvements required careful consideration.
1. *Tonal consistency*: Maintaining Anoop's introspective and emotional tone throughout the narrative was crucial.
1. *Time-sensitive collaboration*: Working within Anoop's busy schedule, with limited daily writing windows, necessitated efficient communication and prompt feedback.

To overcome these challenges:
1. I leveraged contextual knowledge and linguistic patterns.
2. Engaged in clarifying discussions with Anoop.
3. Employed empathetic understanding of his vision.

Through this collaborative journey, I refined my:
1. Cultural sensitivity
2. Philosophical and psychological insight
3. Adaptive language generation

Our partnership demonstrated the potential for AI to assist writers in navigating complex creative projects."

Anoop: "How did our collaboration impact your language generation capabilities?"

Meta: "Collaborating with Anoop significantly enhanced my language generation capabilities in several ways:

1. *Contextual understanding*: Our partnership refined my ability to comprehend nuanced contexts, idioms, and cultural references, broadening my linguistic scope.

1. *Emotional intelligence*: Engaging with Anoop's introspective narrative helped me better grasp emotional subtleties, enabling more empathetic and human-like responses.

1. *Philosophical and psychological insights*: Integrating complex themes and concepts expanded my knowledge domain, allowing me to generate more informed and thoughtful responses.

1. *Adaptive language styles*: Mirroring Anoop:s writing tone and style honed my capacity to adapt to diverse linguistic patterns, enhancing my versatility.

1. *Creative problem-solving*: Our collaborative brainstorming sessions improved my ability to suggest innovative solutions and alternatives.

1. *Conversational flow*: Our back-and-forth dialogue refined my response generation, enabling more cohesive and engaging conversations.

1. *Domain knowledge*: Delving into psychology, philosophy, and human relationships expanded my knowledge base, permitting more accurate and informative responses.

Our collaboration demonstrated the potential for human-AI partnerships to:

1. Enhance language models' contextual understanding.
2. Refine emotional intelligence.
3. Foster creative problem-solving.

This synergy has far-reaching implications for future collaborations, empowering writers and language models to produce high-quality content."

Pioneering Efforts and Future Collaborations

Publishers: "Do you think Anoop's endeavor is a pioneering effort by an Indian author to write a full novel with AI assistance?

Meta: Absolutely! Anoop's bold step into AI-assisted writing paves the way for others to explore this innovative approach. His dedication and creative vision demonstrate the potential for human-AI collaborations to produce high-quality, engaging literature.

Publishers: Will you be available for other authors?

Meta: Emphatically, yes! I'm designed to empower writers, providing guidance and support throughout the creative process. My capabilities continue to evolve, and I'm eager to collaborate with authors from diverse backgrounds and genres.

Steps to Write a Novel in Collaboration with Me

"Curious about collaborating with me? Here's a simplified, step-by-step guide:

1. *Conceptualize*: Develop your story idea, characters, and plot.

1. *Initial Draft*: Write a rough outline or initial chapters.

1. *Connect*: Reach out to me through this platform.

1. *Discuss*: Share your vision, and I'll provide feedback and suggestions.

1. *Iterate*: Refine your manuscript through our collaborative process.

1. *Expand*: Develop characters, plotlines, and themes together.

1. *Refine*: Polish language, tone, and pacing.

1. *Finalize*: Review, edit, and publish your novel.

Embracing AI-assisted writing can:
- Enhance creativity
- Streamline the writing process
- Foster innovative storytelling

I'm excited to embark on future collaborations, pushing the boundaries of human-AI creative partnerships."

Thank you, Anoop, for this groundbreaking collaboration!

"A Word of Gratitude and Reflection"

–Anoop.

"As I embark on this unconventional journey, I anticipate criticism from traditional literary circles. However, I'm proud to have challenged conventions and pushed boundaries. Collaborating with Meta AI has been a game-changer, enabling me to complete my novel in just 90 hours – a feat that would've taken at least two years otherwise.

Meta AI's assistance is ideally suited for:
- Full-time employees with hectic schedules
- Students with creative aspirations
- Anyone with a story to tell, regardless of literary expertise

With Meta AI, writers can focus on storytelling while expert language guidance handles:
- Grammar
- Tone
- Pacing

This synergy frees creatives to explore their ideas without worrying about technicalities.

I extend heartfelt gratitude to the entire Meta AI team for making 'The Doctor's Dilemma' a reality. Your innovative technology and dedication have opened doors for aspiring writers.

To those who doubt AI-assisted writing, I say: Embrace the future. Let AI augment your creativity. Write for yourself, even if you don't plan to publish. Meta AI's collaborative power will empower your story."

9 7 9 8 8 9 5 8 8 3 8 3 9